Too Much Flapdoodle!

Too Much Flapdoodle!

Amy MacDonald

Melanie Kroupa Books
FARRAR STRAUS GIROUX
New York

Distributed in Canada by Douglas & McIntyre Ltd.
Printed in the United States of America
Designed by Jonathan Bartlett
First edition, 2008
10 9 8 7 6 5 4 3 2 1

www.fsgkidsbooks.com

Library of Congress Cataloging-in-Publication Data
MacDonald, Amy.
    Too much flapdoodle / Amy MacDonald ;
[illustrations by Cat Bowman Smith].— 1st ed.
        p.   cm.
    Summary: Twelve-year-old Parker reluctantly goes
to spend the summer with his eccentric great-aunt
and great-uncle on their dilapidated farm, where he
discovers that there is more to life than the latest
game system and the coolest cell phone.
    ISBN-13: 978-0-374-37671-0
    ISBN-10: 0-374-37671-9
    [1. Great-aunts—Fiction.   2. Great-uncles—
Fiction.   3. Country life—Fiction.   4. Farm life—
Fiction.]   I. Smith, Cat Bowman, ill.   II. Title.

PZ7.M1463To 2008
[Fic]—dc22

                                              2007033273

For Monica

Too Much Flapdoodle!

The Funny Farm

"Hurry up, Parker," came his mother's voice from downstairs. "We're going to miss the plane." Then, "Fred, where's your passport?"

Parker sighed, typed a few more words into his blog, and uploaded the entry. Then he turned off the laptop and crammed it into a suitcase already overflowing with video games, comic books, and food. At the last second he remembered his asthma inhaler and grabbed that off his bedside table.

By the time he had dragged, shoved, and bumped the bag down the stairs and into the front hall, he was seriously winded. No one noticed, though. Good Old Dad was busy lugging suitcases out to the waiting car. Good Old Mom was still going on about finding the passport, but it wasn't *his* passport she was concerned about. It was Good Old Dad's. Which made sense, since Dad and Good Old Mom were the ones actually heading to the airport for a trip around the world.

Parker didn't need a passport for where *he* was going. A straitjacket maybe, but not a passport.

———

The farm was nothing like Parker had imagined.

Instead of a gleaming barn with a gleaming silo, sleek race horses cavorting around green fields, some cool tractors and farm machinery, there was only this: a farmhouse—rust red, run-down—its front yard littered with old furniture. The only machines in sight looked like they'd escaped from the junkyard. A swaybacked white nag stood on the swaybacked old veranda—and Parker didn't need to be a horse expert to know that this horse was never going to win any kind of race, except maybe a race to the good old glue factory.

He watched, slouching, from the backseat of the car while Good Old Dad and Good Old Mom stuck their heads in the front door and shouted, "Yoohoo! Maxwells!" They were trying to track down his great-aunt and great-uncle. If the truth must be told, though, at this particular moment Parker didn't really give a rat's tail where Aunt Mattie and Uncle Philbert were. With any luck, they wouldn't show up at all. For the thousandth time he wondered why he had ever let his cousin Simon talk him into this.

"Just about the only thing you can say for sure about that woman," muttered his mother, "is that she is never *where* she is supposed to be *when* she is supposed to be there."

"Shoo! Get away!" shouted Dad, flapping his hands at a brown and white goat that had shambled over for a closer look. It nudged him in the chest with its horns, backing him up against the house, and started explor-

ing his suit pockets. His father raised his hands help-lessly, like someone being mugged.

"I think it's looking for carrots, Fred," said Mom with a nervous laugh. She was wearing her jauntiest clothes—poison green shorts, white sneakers, bright red tennis cap with sun visor. Although she might have been going for the adventure-here-I-come look, Parker thought, she had ended up looking like an ice-cream-sundae-with-a-cherry-on-top. His father, on the other hand, was still wearing his drab business suit, his shiny black shoes. He looked like he was going to the office. And neither of them had achieved that going-on-an-ocean-cruise-and-leaving-our-son-behind-with-decrepit-old-relatives-we-don't-really-know-and-don't-really-like look. But that is exactly what they were doing.

"Those aren't carrots—they're fountain pens! Hey! Giddyup!" yelled Dad. But the goat was clearly on a mission, and moments later Parker heard something that sounded suspiciously like the noise expensive fountain pens make when being eaten by a goat.

"Don't look at me," said Mom. "I told you all along this was a dreadful idea."

Parker couldn't have agreed more. Scrolling the car window up, he replaced his earbuds and adjusted the drop-down TV screen that hung from the ceiling of the cavernous SUV.

"Darling . . ." Mom had opened the car door. "Sweetie darling, don't sit in here with the window shut. You'll get heatstroke. Come join us."

Parker pretended not to hear. He turned the volume up, fast-forwarded the movie to the part where the Earth and most of the solar system exploded in a deeply satisfying fireball, and tried hard not to think about how boring and awful this summer was going to be.

Just when his parents seemed about ready to give up and leave, just when they seemed *this* close to calling it all off, there was a noise from a field behind the barn, and an ancient motorcycle appeared, making an unearthly racket as it bounded through a scraggly field of unmown hay. Parker got out of the car for a better look. Yes, it was Uncle Philbert sitting in the motorcycle's sidecar, gripping the edge and holding something

in his lap while Aunt Mattie drove, wisps of white hair streaming behind her. She brought the motorbike to a lurching halt before Parker and his startled parents.

When the dust had settled, Uncle Philbert let go of his death grip on the sidecar, unfolded his long legs, and stepped out. Parker could see now that the object he was clutching was a lamb. His great-uncle paid no attention to Mom and Dad, but turned to look admiringly at Aunt Mattie.

"Matilda," he said as he pulled several burs from his hair and his droopy silver mustache, "I reckon you might have set a new speed record just now. Next time, however"—he spat out some hayseeds that had gotten stuck between his teeth—"remind me to wear a helmet."

"Well, it *was* an emergency," said Aunt Mattie, calmly removing an old-fashioned pair of leather goggles and dismounting. She smiled at Mom and Dad. "We had to rescue a poor motherless lamb, which is why we're a bit late."

"Please don't apologize on our account," Mom began.

"I wouldn't dream of it," said Aunt Mattie with a smile. "I'm a firm believer in being late. Now if you'll excuse me, I have to go heat up some milk." And she scurried—pretty darn fast for such an old lady—into the house.

"Thinks she's Dale Earnhardt," said Uncle Philbert, shaking his head as he watched her go. Then he turned to Parker, and skipping right past the Hello-how-are-you-young-man part of the conversation, he thrust the lamb into Parker's arms. "Buster," he said. "What do you think of that?"

"Huh?" sputtered Parker, holding the tiny animal at arm's length.

"As a name. For the lamb. Kind of suits her, doncha think?" He bent to pick up Parker's bag. "Well, come on," he said, addressing Parker's parents for the first time. "Time's a wastin'. Who's up for some hot milk?"

Parker watched his parents trudge into the farmhouse and looked down at Buster. "Welcome to the funny farm," he said with a sigh.

Parker had protested. No way could he feed a baby lamb. But had anyone listened? No, they had not.

"Sure you can," Uncle Philbert insisted, thrusting the baby bottle full of warm milk into his hand. "You don't need to worry about Buster peeing on you. She's wearing a diaper." She was, which only made it worse.

"But I . . . I'm . . . allergic. To animal hair. My doctor says—"

"You're allergic to wool?" Uncle Philbert eyed him skeptically.

"No, of course not, I . . ." Parker stopped, realizing he'd been tricked. Wool. Duh. People weren't allergic to wool.

And so it was that he found himself sitting in a rocking chair, bottle-feeding a baby lamb in a cloth diaper. He was determined to keep his face in a scowl and not to pay any attention to the way Buster stared up at him with her enormous and adoring brown eyes. The few times he surreptitiously stroked the soft fur at her

throat, he frowned even harder so that if anyone saw him, it would be clear he was just trying to keep the silly beast from drooling milk all over his pants. *If anyone at school ever finds out about this,* he reminded himself, *I am so dead.*

His parents seemed maddeningly unaware of just how put upon he was feeling. Good Old Mom was perched nervously on the edge of the lumpy sofa like she was afraid that something—some essence of Aunt Mattie and Uncle Philbert—might rub off on her. Dad was perched on the edge of Aunt Mattie's overstuffed armchair like he was worried that if he relaxed back into its comfortable depths he might never get out again. When he thought no one was looking, he snuck glances at his watch. Both parents balanced full cups of tea on their knees that they obviously had no intention of drinking.

On the same lumpy sofa lounged Uncle Philbert, clearly unworried by lambs, cats, cat hair, lamb hair, dust, or any of the other things the couch was covered in at the moment. He was rabbiting on about some sort of crop he'd just cut down or raked up or whatever it was you did to crops. Every now and then, when he paused to draw breath, Dad or Mom would say "Oh really?" or "Is that so?"

"Cake is ready," interrupted Aunt Mattie, wafting into the room from the kitchen on a cloud of fresh-baked-cake aroma and bearing the oddest-looking cake Parker had ever seen. It was shaped something like a tall mushroom, covered in frosting the color of his mother's jaunty red cap. It reminded Parker of the part in *Alice in Wonderland* before the Mad Hatter's tea party, where Alice finds a giant mushroom, and if you ate a piece from one side it made you larger and a piece from the other side made you smaller. Or something like that. In fact, Parker recalled dimly, as Buster finished the bottle and started trying to suck his fingers, there was even a baby pig in the story, a pig that everyone treated like a human baby.

"Won't cake spoil Parker's appetite for lunch?" Mom protested faintly. Whether it was lunchtime or teatime was hard to tell, as a grandfather clock in the corner confused everyone by striking twenty-five. Twenty-five o'clock.

Definitely the Mad Hatter's tea party, thought Parker as Dad checked his watch again and Uncle Philbert took Buster and settled her in a playpen he'd set up in the corner.

Aunt Mattie seemed not to have heard Mom. "Who'd like some coffee cake?" she asked, looking around.

"What an unusual concoction!" said Mom in her bright and happy voice. "What makes it a coffee cake?"

"It's a coffee cake because I bake it in a coffee can," Aunt Mattie replied.

"How . . . quaint," said Mom. "A coffee can."

Holding the cake knife sideways, Aunt Mattie began slicing the top off the bright red mushroom. Parker couldn't help objecting. "That top slice has *all* the frosting."

"So it does." Aunt Mattie placed the top piece on a plate and continued cutting sideways slices. "I find— don't you?—that either people like frosting or they don't. With a coffee cake, people who like frosting get all the frosting. And people who don't like frosting don't have to have any."

"I like frosting," Parker announced. He ignored his mother's frown.

"There, you see what I mean?" said Aunt Mattie, passing out the slices and giving him the first one.

"Parker really shouldn't have frosting. Too much sugar. And red food dye," said Good Old Mom, putting down her cake in a way that made it obvious she thought it was toxic. "He's very delicate."

Good Old Dad rolled his eyes at this. "Honey," he said, "a little food dye won't kill him. He's not—"

12

"He's a fragile flower," his mother insisted, smoothing an imaginary wrinkle out of her pressed shorts. "Very delicate."

Parker took advantage of his parents' argument to wolf down his slice of cake and then snag his mother's plate without anyone noticing. The cake was delicious, although it was definitely from the side of the mushroom that made you larger. Parker slid a hand under his T-shirt and undid the top button of his jeans—jeans that were meant to be baggy but were painfully tight and getting tighter.

"Now, as I was saying," Mom continued, "I am just a teensy-weensy bit worried about all the animal hair. You see, Parker suffers dreadfully from asthma."

At this moment, Dad's pocket began making a loud, howling noise that was all too familiar to Parker. His father leaped to his feet at the same time as Aunt Mattie and Uncle Philbert.

"What's that?" asked Aunt Mattie.

"Someone sat on a cat," Philbert cried, looking around in alarm. He began checking under the sofa cushions, scattering cats in all directions.

"That? Oh, that's just Fred's cell phone," said Mom with a laugh. "He promised me he was going to leave it home, but . . ." She sighed and shrugged.

Dad had flicked the phone open, silencing the dying-cat noise. Turning his back on everyone, he began speaking in the rapid-fire voice he reserved for talking to his office.

"No, Plimpton," he said. "I told you, the development rights are a deal breaker. You go back to the drawing board and . . ."

Uncle Philbert, clutching a sofa cushion to his chest, muttered something that sounded to Parker like "And I thought *I* was the rudest man in the world."

"Mostly it's just dust that causes it—the asthma," continued Mom. "Dust and exercise. He should avoid both at all costs. He's allergic to pollen, so he shouldn't go outdoors when it's . . . when there's pollen. Also, did I mention, no sugar or red food dye?" She looked pointedly at the mushroom cake. "Those are very bad for you. Now, as to animal hair, I don't *think* he's allergic, but you can't be too careful. He's a very sensitive boy." She brushed her hand absently against the sofa as she talked, and a small cloud of black, orange, brown, white, and gray animal hair sifted into the air, mixed with a fair amount of dust.

"I dusted his bedroom and removed the carpet and curtains, just as you requested—" began Aunt Mattie, but at that moment Parker started coughing violently. He felt his face turn bright red as his throat closed and he wheezed and gasped for air.

"Oh my God he's having an asthma attack!" Mom screeched. "It's the cat hair. The dust! Fred, get the inhaler! The pills! Get some water!" She dashed out of the room toward the car while Aunt Mattie scurried into the kitchen. Dad, still shouting into the cell phone, plugged a finger into his other ear and walked to the far end of the room.

"Raise your hands over your head, son," Uncle Philbert instructed. Parker did as he was told. Uncle

Philbert came calmly over and pounded him on the back a few times. The coughing stopped.

Mom rushed back into the room just as Dad snapped his phone shut and Aunt Mattie appeared with a glass of water, looking alarmed. Parker used his inhaler and held out his hand for the pill. He did it all without protest, wheezing once or twice more.

Uncle Philbert took the glass of water from Aunt Mattie, saying under his breath as he did so, "Dobon't woborroby." As he passed the glass of water to Parker, he did something even stranger.

He winked at him.

The goodbyes had been long and painful. Good Old Mom cried, of course. She said they'd be back for him on a date that seemed so impossibly far in the future that Parker promptly forgot it. Then she hugged him two more times and reminded him yet again to brush his teeth and not eat any crunchy food because of his braces but always clean his plate, and to avoid dust and exercise and never go *anywhere* without his in-haler. And while she was explaining that they would be completely out of touch on the cruise ship and Aunt Mattie was reassuring his mother for the third time about the cat hair, Dad, standing by the driver's side of the car, motioned him over.

"So, this is goodbye," he said.

"Yeah," said Parker. There was a pause while Good Old Dad absentmindedly polished the tip of one shiny black shoe on the back of his pant leg, rubbing off the driveway dust. He seemed to suddenly think of something and, reaching into his suit pocket, pulled out a slim leather wallet. He slid five crisp new bills from the wallet and handed them to Parker.

"Here ya go, buddy. That's for emergencies. Or to buy yourself something gnarly."

Parker looked at the bills. Five hundred dollars. "Thanks," he mumbled. He wished his father wouldn't call him buddy and try to talk like a teenager. It made Parker cringe. Dad wasn't his buddy, nor was he a teenager. He was a big, fancy hotshot lawyer.

"Well, so long."

Parker stuck out a hand to say goodbye at the same moment that Dad raised his hand to high-five him. Parker responded by raising his hand to high-five his father at the same instant that his father lowered his in order to shake. Then they did the same thing again, but in reverse. Dad stopped and grinned at him. It was a rare grin, not one of the usual distracted smiles he would shoot at Parker while he was on the phone or at the computer, but one that traveled all the way to his eyes and back down again. It came and went in a flash, but it caused little crow's-feet to form at the corners of his eyes.

"Okay, big guy," he said, solving the awkward handshake problem by clapping Parker on the shoulder. "Have a good vacation."

As the car pulled away Parker heard the sound of his father's cell phone ringing again in the front seat. Moments later, he saw something looking suspiciously like a cell phone fly out of the passenger window and land with a splash in a small duck pond beside the road.

Watching his parents drive off, Parker was overcome with a sudden pang of dismay. He began running after the car, crying out and waving his arms. The car rounded the bend in the driveway without pause, leaving Parker doubled over in the middle of the dirt road, hands on knees, gasping for breath. Uncle Philbert caught up to him and put a consoling arm around his shoulder.

"Never mind," he said. "In a few days you'll stop missin' them."

Parker stared at the ground, trying to breathe more evenly. "I don't miss them," he gasped. "I left my . . . stupid iPod . . . in the stupid . . . *stupid* backseat."

Way Too Exciting

The first thing Parker unpacked was his laptop, but looking around the small bedroom that was to be his for the next six weeks, he could see no place to connect to the Internet. Six weeks without the Internet? He shuddered, then tucked the laptop under his arm and went downstairs.

In the kitchen, Uncle Philbert was reading a book called *The Gentle Art of Pig Farming* and Aunt Mattie was clearing dishes into a long sink made of black stone that looked like a horse's watering trough.

"I suppose it would be silly to ask if you have wireless?" said Parker, even though it was more likely that his great-aunt and great-uncle kept an elephant in the basement than a wireless Internet modem.

"Wireless?" said Aunt Mattie. "Of course we do. Right there."

She wiped her hands on her apron and pointed to a strange object on the kitchen counter: a battered wooden thing the size of a breadbox, its front covered in a weird shiny cloth, with dials and knobs running along the bottom. Parker put his laptop down and stared at it. He'd never seen a modem before, but he felt sure that it ought to look a bit more, well, modem-y.

"How does it work?"

"How?" Aunt Mattie seemed baffled by the question. "Why, you turn it on here, of course." She turned the left-hand knob until it clicked, and a dim light lit up a double row of numbers. "And you tune it here." She indicated the other knob.

Uncle Philbert rattled his newspaper and shook his head sadly. "And here I thought you young people knew all about *tech-nol-logee*."

A sudden hissing and crackling came from the breadbox, followed by a faint but growing sound that Parker recognized as country music. He jumped as if he'd been bitten by a snake.

"It's a . . . It's not a . . . It's a *radio*!"

"Yes, dear. That's what I said. A wireless. I guess you young people today call it a radio."

Parker was still trying to make sense of this when Uncle Philbert stood up and announced that he was going to take a nap while the two of them "tea kittled" up the dirty dishes. Afterward they could play Scrabble.

Scrabble? Parker looked at him in disbelief. "I don't think so," he said, edging for the exit. This would be the moment to escape back to his room and dig out his Game Boy. "I'm gonna go, uh, take a nap, too. And, well, a nap *and* Scrabble would be just *way* too much excitement for one day. My doctor says—"

Aunt Mattie interrupted him before he could get out the door. "Would you druther wash or dry?" she asked, holding out a scrub brush in one hand and a drying-up towel in the other. Then, before he could answer, she turned to Uncle Philbert with a small frown. "And since when do you take a nap in the middle of the day?"

"I have to take a nap in the middle of the *day* because if I took a nap in the middle of the *night*, it wouldn't be a *nap*, would it?" said Uncle Philbert. Then he sidled out of the kitchen.

Parker glanced at his great-aunt and then at the dirty dishes. She had to be kidding. He had no idea how to wash—or dry—dishes.

At home, he was in the habit of walking away from the table without even clearing his place. Sure, he knew there was a dishwasher somewhere, but how it got filled and emptied was not something he'd ever worried about. He was pretty sure that the cleaning woman had something to do with it. Beyond that, as far as he knew, he dirtied a dish, and it magically reappeared later on the shelf, clean and ready for him to use again. It was the same with his laundry: drop dirty clothes on the floor, and like magic they reappeared in his dresser, all clean and folded. It was sort of like there was a laundry fairy. Or a dish fairy.

"Where's the dishwasher?" He glanced around the kitchen.

"You're it!" said Aunt Mattie with a smile.

No way. Everyone had a dishwasher. Then he spied it, next to the sink. "Here it is," he said, tugging on the front of it. The door folded down, and there it was: the dishwasher. He pointed to it with a smirk.

"Sorry to disappoint," said Mattie. "It's full."

Parker looked more closely. The dishwasher was indeed full—but not of dishes. Pads of paper, dictionaries, and books were stacked in the places where dishes usually went. In the silverware holder were pens, pencils, scissors, a ruler, even a quill pen.

"Makes a fine desk," said Aunt Mattie, replacing *The Gentle Art of Pig Farming* on the lower rack next to a copy of *Huckleberry Finn* and shutting the door. At that moment, an indescribable sound filled the kitchen. It was the kind of noise an electric blender would make if someone threw a handful of gravel into it.

"What was *that*?" gasped Parker.

"That," Aunt Mattie said, laughing, "is the sound the dishwasher made just before it gave up the ghost for good. It made a big impression on Runcible, who was sitting on top of it at the time."

Parker followed Aunt Mattie's gaze and recognized a large gray parrot perched in a cage in one corner of the kitchen. "Whoa. Runcible made that noise?"

"She's very clever at imitating machines."

"But dishwashers don't sound like *that*!"

"Not usually. But that dishwasher is twenty years old, and everything—humans, animals, and machines—we all have an expiration date, so to speak. When it started feeling poorly, I was happy to let it die a peaceful death. But your Uncle Philbert is a stubborn old man and he decided to 'fix' it for me. Dear Bertie. He might have the magic touch with animals, but he is death on machines of any kind. One touch from him, just a *touch*, and anything mechanical is completely jizzicked."

She saw Parker frown at the word. "Ruined," she explained. "Ready for the junkyard. Anyway, the next time I turned it on, it made that dreadful noise, and when I opened the door . . . Well, I don't think there was anything left in there bigger than a marble."

Parker was dumbfounded. "Why didn't you just get a new one?"

"Oh my. They cost such a great deal of money."

"You should do what my mom does, then."

"What's that, dear?"

"She lets the cleaning woman do the dishes."

For some reason, Aunt Mattie seemed to think that was the wittiest remark she'd ever heard. "Oh, Parker." She sighed happily. "Who'd have guessed you had such a sense of humor? The cleaning woman!" Still giggling, she passed him the scrub brush. "Now then, let me show you what to do. First, you've got to scrape the food off into—"

"Wait," said Parker. "I know this part." He did, too. He loved stuffing things into the garbage disposal in their kitchen. Once, he'd put a whole box of wooden matches down it and flicked it on, just to see what would happen. That had been very cool. He searched the black slate sink. "Where's the pig?"

"Pig?" Aunt Mattie looked baffled. "You mean Oswald? He's in the barn, of course."

"No. The *pig*. Don't you have a pig for food scraps?"

"We do. But, as I said, he's in the barn. We put his scraps in this bucket here."

It slowly dawned on Parker that Aunt Mattie had no

idea that he was talking about a garbage disposal. He stifled a snicker. "Right," he said, scraping a plate into the bucket. "A pig. Oink. Oink." No one at home would believe this.

When they finished, Parker tried for a second time to sneak upstairs, but he ran into Uncle Philbert, who was donning a pair of work gloves.

"Here," Uncle Philbert said, handing a second pair to Parker. "We might as well get to work."

"Work?" said Parker, staring blankly at the gloves.

"Yep. Time for chores."

"Eat my shorts!" said Runcible.

"No," said Aunt Mattie, bending over her cage and speaking slowly and loudly. " 'Time for chores.' Not 'Eat my shorts.' "

"Chores?" echoed Parker. Simon hadn't said any-thing about doing chores when he'd stayed here.

"If you're gonna repeat everything I say, it's gonna take twice as long. Let's go. Wood don't split itself, you know."

"I . . . I can't do chores," objected Parker. This was perfectly true. He didn't do chores. Parker was vaguely aware that most kids his age did something to earn their allowance: made their beds, raked leaves, took out the trash. But ever since he could remember, there'd always been a cleaning woman or a nanny or a lawn-service guy who did all that. All he had to do to collect his fifty-dollar-a-week allowance was, basically, show up for the occasional meal.

"Why not?"

"Well . . . I . . . The dust. The animal hair. My asthma. Allergies. My doctor says—"

"Nuts!" said Uncle Philbert.

Even Aunt Matilda seemed stunned by this remark. "But, Bertie," she said, "you saw for yourself during tea, with the cat hair—"

"What I saw," said Uncle Philbert, "wasn't asthma. Or allergies. I saw a boy chokin' on a cake crumb. Ain't that right, son? You were busy scarfin' down that cake so fast, some of it went down the wrong way. Can't say as I blame you. That cake was some tasty."

Parker said nothing. There was nothing he could say. He was busted and he knew it. Uncle Philbert took down a pair of baseball caps from a peg by the door.

"You'll need this," he said, putting one on and handing the other to Parker. "Weather is mortifying today."

Despite himself, Parker was kind of excited by the thought of being allowed to run a wood splitter. He'd seen one once, in an ultra-gory movie. It had been a sweet, loud machine that slammed each length of wood headfirst into a sharp metal blade, slicing it violently in half lengthwise.

"Where's the splitting machine?" he asked, making sure his voice didn't betray the slightest feeling of eagerness.

"You're lookin' at it," said Uncle Philbert, entering a toolshed. He shouldered a sledgehammer and held out a shiny steel wedge to Parker.

"What?" Parker exclaimed. "That's not a splitter." He reached for the wedge. "That's just a stupid—"

The wedge was so unexpectedly heavy that Parker dropped it straight onto his big toe, point first.

"Ow!" he shouted, hopping up and down and clutching his throbbing foot. "Ow! Oh, I think it's broken. I broke my foot! I broke my freakin' foot!" He sat down on the toolshed floor, took off his sandal, and rubbed his toes.

Uncle Philbert watched him for a while. When it was quite clear to him that Parker hadn't broken his foot, just kind of stunned it, he said, "Let's go."

"You're kidding," said Parker. "I need to go to the

hospital. I need a doctor. I can't even walk." Wait until he told his parents about this! His mother would never believe it. Making him work with a broken foot! If he'd been at home, his parents would have whisked him straight off to the emergency room for X-rays.

Astonishingly, Uncle Philbert just stood there, holding out the steel wedge.

So Parker made a decision. He'd had enough. He'd been tricked into feeding a diaper-wearing lamb and doing dishes, but this was going too far. He stood up and shot Uncle Philbert a look that he hoped conveyed both contempt and suffering. "I'm going to go lie down," he said. Then, with a hugely exaggerated limp, he headed back into the house.

He needed some quality time with his Game Boy, and nothing else was going to get in his way.

Marooned!

Parker had just made it to Level 8 of Indy 500, vaporizing his racing Porsche in a spectacular crash, when he had his first happy thought since he'd arrived: maybe there was no Internet, but there was no logical reason why he couldn't play video games sixteen hours a day for the rest of the summer. Aunt Mattie and Uncle Philbert had left him alone all afternoon and evening, interrupting him just twice. The first time was to bring him a bowl with two goldfish in it that Philbert claimed needed "cheering up" because they were bored to death sitting in the kitchen looking at old people. The second time was to let him know supper was ready. At five o'clock. Parker had responded that he wasn't hungry, and Aunt Mattie had simply nodded and gone away.

Clearly Aunt Mattie and Uncle Philbert weren't the types to burst into his room and demand to know what he was up to, the way his mother did. Maybe here, at least, no one would bug him to stop "wasting his life" playing video games. Come to think of it, his great-aunt and great-uncle had probably never even heard of video games. If they asked him what he was doing, he could tell them he was honing his computer skills. Yeah, preparing for the SAT.

Parker snickered, thinking how close he had come to spending the summer at SAT camp, and then inserted a new horse-racing game cartridge he'd bought called Triple Crown. Minutes later he cursed as the low-battery signal appeared. No problem. He had fresh batteries—a huge pack of double A's—and a plug as well. He finished off the last of the Cheesios he'd brought with him, tossed the bag in the vague direction of the wastebasket, and emptied his suitcase onto the floor.

But the batteries weren't there. Nor was the plug. With a horrible sinking feeling, he remembered where they all were: in his backpack. And the backpack was in the backseat of the stupid SUV along with his stupid iPod. He picked up the Game Boy and looked at it for a long, angry moment before he flung it at the bed as hard as he could.

He missed the bed. But not the brass headboard. The Game Boy splattered against the metal and showered the bed with plastic shrapnel.

Well, this was craptastic. Parker swept the plastic shards off the bed and climbed on top of it. He lay there, staring at the cracks in the ceiling for a long time, trying to remember how he had gotten himself into this mess. He was pretty sure it was all Simon's fault.

Yeah, it was definitely his younger cousin's fault. Simon the goody-goody, in his dweeberrific button-down shirts and neatly pressed pants, had somehow convinced Parker that their weirdo great-aunt and great-uncle were cool—that he, too, would have "fun" if he ever went to visit them.

Parker searched his soul for a brief moment. No, it wasn't fair to put all the blame on Simon. Some of the blame also belonged to . . . his parents.

From the moment they all first met Aunt Mattie and Uncle Philbert—at Simon's birthday party that spring—it had been clear that his straitlaced parents did not approve of them. Good Old Mom and Dad had packed up and left in a huff, halfway through the party, just when things started to get out of control in an interesting sort of way, what with the belching and the cats and parrots getting into the act. At the time, Parker didn't quite know what to make of his odd relatives. But later, when the chips were down, he figured that any two people who got under his parents' skin that much had to have *something* going for them.

That's why he had insisted on it when his parents announced a few weeks later that they were taking a round-the-world cruise from Alaska to Greenland this summer to celebrate some big romantic wedding anniversary. Just the two of them.

"You're taking all that time off from work?" Parker was floored. His father worked *all the time*. He loved work. He worked when he was at the office, and he worked when he was at home. He worked on weekends, and he worked on vacations. Oh, wait. That's right. He never took *vacations*. He never even took sick days. He just worked *all the time*.

The question seemed to surprise his father. "Well, I—"

"Yes," Mom said firmly. "He has lots of vacation time saved up. And he's not even taking his cell phone with him. Are you, Fred?"

"What about me?" asked Parker.

"You!" said Dad, producing a glossy brochure with a flourish. "We are sending *you* to . . . computer camp!" The place was called Cram-alot, or some such name. Its motto: "We cram a lot of *fun* into math and science!" The brochure showed scenes of happy math-team-and-chess-club kids clustering around computer screens. Looking on with big smiles as adults pointed to complicated math formulas on blackboards. Reading computer printouts with impish grins. "Have *fun* while you learn!"

"Simon went there last year. He loved it," said Mom.

"Well, Simon *would* love it, wouldn't he?"

"And then he won some sort of prize at the Science Fair," his father added. Trust Good Old Dad not to miss a chance to point out how perfectly perfect Saint Simon was.

Well, big freakin' deal. Parker could have won a prize at the Science Fair, too, if he cared about that sort of thing. Which he didn't.

"I hate computers."

"Nonsense," chirped Mom. "You spend hours on that computer of yours."

"Yeah, but—" He stopped himself. His parents had this fond, crazy idea that he was some kind of computer genius. How could he—or should he—explain to

30

them the difference between *working* on a computer and *playing* on a computer? He wasn't designing software or Web pages like Simon. No, he was playing Minesweeper and Doom, IMing, and surfing sites like LameJokes.com. Mostly, though, he was checking eBay for ways to add to his comic book collection and his stash of video games. Wasting his life, to put it bluntly. He decided to say nothing. He might as well let his parents think he was good at *something*.

"It will look good on your college applications," added Dad. "Says here they help prepare you for the SAT, too."

"And it's *never* too soon for college," snarked Parker. The sarcasm, however, was completely lost on his father, who simply nodded in agreement. Parker looked from one parent to the other in astonishment. "Mom. Dad. I'm not even in eighth grade. I don't have to think about SATs and college for *years*."

"As you said, it's never too soon to start," Dad stated flatly. "Unless, of course, you have a better idea?"

"I do, actually," Parker blurted out. His parents stared at him. "I . . . I want to go stay with Aunt Mattie and Uncle Philbert. They invited me."

"*What?*" barked Dad.

Something about the very surprise in his father's voice made Parker sit up straighter. He probably thought Parker couldn't hack it at the farm, away from all his creature comforts. "Yeah," he said, with real conviction now. "I really, *really* want to visit them."

"Never!" said Mom, recovering her power of speech. "I can't imagine anything worse. We've been through

31

this already. Dirt and dust and filthy animals. You will ruin your health. You are far too delicate."

"Simon went there, and *he* loved it," Parker retorted, pleased to be able to throw their own words back in their faces. They couldn't say no if Little Mr. Perfect had liked it. "And that's what I want to do." He shot Dad a defiant look. "I'm not going to Camp Crap-alot. No way."

"Fred—" his mother began.

But Parker's father held up a hand. He looked at Parker and seemed to be sizing him up. "Are you sure?"

"Positive," asserted Parker, who had never been less sure of anything in his life.

"Okay, then," said his father. "The farm it is." He then turned to Parker's mother. "No, honey. There's no use discussing it. The boy's made up his mind."

That was the end of the discussion.

And the beginning of Parker's sense of dismay. Just what had he gotten himself into?

Or, rather, what had his *parents* gotten him into? Because, let's be honest, what kinds of parents leave their kid with two certified lunatics for the summer?

Parker patted his jeans pocket, checking for his cell phone and his asthma inhaler, the two items he never left home without. It was a gesture he repeated many times a day, finding a certain comfort in knowing they were there if he needed them.

To be honest, he needed the inhaler less and less these days. In fact, he hadn't had a real asthma attack in months. (Plenty of fake ones, since he'd learned ages ago that nothing got his parents' attention like a wheeze or two.) But the memory of the real thing was vivid enough and scary enough that he couldn't imagine going anywhere without the inhaler in his pocket. As for the cell phone, it was a lifeline. There was no other way to put it.

He slid the cell phone out of its special pocket and turned it on. *No service.* He tried again, nearer the window. Nothing. He couldn't understand how his dad's cell phone could work when his didn't. Then he remembered that the phone he'd insisted his father buy him for Christmas—the "must-have" phone that cost a small fortune and could do everything short of scrambling eggs—that phone had used a different phone service from his dad's.

Well, wasn't this just craptacular. Cell Phone Service Black Hole. That's where he was going to be spending the rest of the summer. He couldn't call anyone. He couldn't text anyone. He couldn't e-mail. He was completely cut off from the rest of the world. Marooned. Hey, there was an idea—maybe they could make a reality TV show around him: *Tune in next week on* Marooned, *when Parker gets to vote one person off the Funny Farm—himself!*

The person he most wanted to call was Simon. He wanted to call and ask him, *Exactly what part of this place is fun?* But he couldn't even do that.

One of the goldfish on his bedside table gave him a fishy yawn. It was 9:04 p.m.

"You think *your* life is boring?" Parker snapped. "Try mine! No iPod, no Internet, no cell phone, no Game Boy, no—" Wait a minute—he still had his Wii and tons of DVDs. He just had to find the TV, and then he could stay up all night watching movies and playing games. He sat straight up in bed.

Parker had been amazed to discover there wasn't a television set anywhere in his room. But since his great-aunt and great-uncle had gone to bed—at the amazing hour of nine o'clock—he ought to be able to use their set. He crept down the darkened stairs, narrowly avoiding tripping over several cats. The ground floor was a dim obstacle course consisting of old junk stacked in heaps. He searched the entire downstairs—living room, front parlor, kitchen, pantry. He checked inside the kitchen cabinets in case they had one of those little TV sets mounted there, like his parents did, so they could watch TV during meals. He ransacked closets and cupboards. One closet was full of old sports equipment (most of it missing some important part, like the strings to the tennis rackets). Two cupboards were crammed to overflowing with the kind of clutter that would drive his mother mad: empty jam jars, old yogurt containers, and vintage phonograph records. But did he find even one measly television set? No. *No TV anywhere at all.*

His prowling around had woken Buster, and she stood in her pen, making soft bleating sounds. "Quit it," said Parker, trying to sound stern and stroking her head. Buster looked at him with her huge dark eyes and then took Parker's index finger into her mouth and began sucking hungrily. Startled, Parker snatched his hand away, and Buster promptly staggered backward and plopped down with a look of surprise on her face. Parker couldn't help laughing, Buster looked so comical sitting on her hindquarters in her diapers, legs all splayed. He set her carefully back on her wobbly feet. "There you go, you complete doofus," he whispered, then leaned in and held his index finger to his lips. "Now could you try not to wake up the entire United States of America? Please?"

Buster's hunger reminded Parker that he had missed supper. He went back into the kitchen to find something to eat. In one corner was a round-shouldered little fridge, in another a cast-iron, wood-fired cookstove. At the far end a door led into a pantry. The cookstove seemed to be used mainly as a trash incinerator. (At one point Uncle Philbert had emptied most of the day's mail into it—unopened.) The pantry shelves were bare except for what Parker thought of as "old people" food: canisters labeled Flour or Oats or Dried Beans. Bowls of apples. Tins of cat food. Even the old fridge was mostly empty: Pickles. Eggs. Vegetables. Not a bite to eat anywhere.

He sat glumly in the empty kitchen, playing with the ring tones he'd downloaded on his cell phone. Or, rather, the ring tones that all the other kids in his class had downloaded for him. For a short while there, when he'd first brought the phone to school, he'd been the most popular boy in his class—the only one with the must-have phone. He hadn't objected when Jensen and Burrows had snatched it from him at lunch and started playing with it, downloading different stuff, taking stupid pictures—close-ups of their mouths full of mashed potatoes—making crank phone calls to far-off countries, tossing the fragile phone back and forth and laughing like fools. He hadn't objected. In fact, he'd loved each minute of his short-lived popularity. Even after the phone bill came, and Dad freaked. It had been worth it.

He finally put the phone down with a sigh. It was nine-thirty and there was nothing to do but go to bed. How was he going to survive the summer? This place was worse than jail. He knew from watching cop shows that even jails had TVs.

He would have to make sure his parents were sorry about leaving him behind, about letting him stay in this prison. He'd show them. He would go back to his room and stay there for the entire summer. No, actually, he'd stay in his *bed* the entire summer. He would eat and sleep, and do nothing else. He would just become a human vegetable. Maybe he wouldn't even eat. Maybe he would just lie in bed and waste away until his parents had to leave their stupid cruise and come home and put him in the hospital—then they would be sorry they had ruined his summer vacation and nearly killed him.

He was heading back to bed when he noticed a blanket chest in the hall that he hadn't checked out yet. He cleared the clutter off the top and opened it. Inside were *National Geographic* magazines from the 1940s, crossword-puzzle books that had been completely filled out, and a stack of photo albums. He picked one up and opened it at random, to a photo of a gangly young man and a slim woman atop a shiny new tractor with a Just Married sign slung across it. She wore a long white dress with what looked like work boots, and he wore a suit that looked way too big for him. With an uncomfortable start, Parker realized it must be his great-aunt and great-uncle. It did something unsettling to his view of the world to think that they could ever have been *that* young. Hastily replacing the album, he was about to close the chest when he saw, at the very bottom, something colorful that looked suspiciously like . . . He dug down carefully and—yes, it was! Dozens and dozens of Batman comics. Ancient ones, it's true, but still: comic books. Ones he'd never read.

Well, maybe the summer wouldn't be a *total* loss. He grabbed an armload of the comics. "To the Bat Cave!" he muttered as he trudged back to his room.

The Curious Incident of the Popcorn at Midnight

Midnight. Parker was still awake. The problem now was that he was ravenous. The cake and Cheesios he'd eaten hours ago were not going to hold him till morning, and he couldn't face eating any more of the candy he'd brought. Remembering the five hundred dollars in his pocket, he had a sudden brainstorm: "Mama Gina's makes house calls." He could call and have pizza delivered right to his door. There was probably even enough money to order out every single night he was here. Sweet!

During his search of the living room, he'd noticed a strange-looking phone in a cardboard box. Sneaking downstairs, he dug it out again, lifted the heavy curved receiver, and held it to his ear. No dial tone. In vain he looked for a Talk button. Then he saw a strange cord sticking out of the bottom that ended in a big square plug with four round prongs. It clearly needed to be plugged in *somewhere*, but though Parker tried and tried, he couldn't make it fit into a single electrical outlet.

So much for Mama Gina's. He was about to go back to bed when he remembered that he had a giant Mega-Pak of microwave popcorn in his suitcase. He retrieved it quickly, his stomach growling and mouth watering in happy anticipation. Ripping the box open, he pulled out a bag and then stood there, stupidly, in the middle of the kitchen looking around. *Idiot.* Of course there was no microwave.

Parker held up the bag, with its tantalizing picture of a big bowl of buttery popcorn. This felt like the final straw, and he was briefly tempted to heave the bag through the nearest window. Instead, he shoved it into the cookstove. Then he crammed in the rest of the Mega-Pak. He didn't care that the heavy iron door crashed loudly when he shut it. He didn't care who he woke up. He was, in a word, fed up. And he didn't care who knew it.

There is almost no limit to the amount of havoc a giant Mega-Pak of microwave popcorn can create inside even the sturdiest cast-iron stove, provided just the right amount of heat is applied. And there must have been just the right amount of coals, left over from dinner, to apply just the right amount of heat.

Parker was already back in his own bedroom when he heard the first warning sounds coming from the kitchen: a tiny muffled explosion, followed by a second and a third, widely spaced, like the first gentle fat flakes of snow that announce the coming of a major blizzard. By the time Parker decided to go back to

investigate, the noise had grown to a deafening cre-
scendo. He opened the door to the kitchen, and his jaw
sagged in disbelief.

The popcorn had blown the lid off the cookstove and
forced open the door to the firebox. Like sparks from
an erupting volcano, hot kernels were shooting out the
top of the stove and pinging off the ceiling. A vast lava-
like wave of popcorn oozed out the door of the firebox,
creating deep piles on the kitchen floor.

Parker had no idea how long he'd been standing
there, open-mouthed, by the time Uncle Philbert appeared, clad in long johns, clutching a baseball bat in
one hand, a flashlight in the other. Aunt Mattie was
close behind him. Parker hung his head. He was going
to get royally reamed out for making such a god-awful
Mega-mess, for destroying the stove, for waking up

people in the middle of the night. He knew he deserved it, so he clamped his mouth shut, put on his best scowl, and prepared to deny everything.

Uncle Philbert surveyed the scene silently, then turned to Aunt Mattie. "Can you believe it?" he said at last, raising his voice to be heard above the exploding popcorn. "Burglars again." He lowered the baseball bat and turned to Parker, his expression deadpan. "Happens all the time."

"Yes," said Aunt Mattie. "People are always breaking into the house and making popcorn. It's a real nuisance. We'll have to start locking our door at night."

"I'll get some snow shovels," said Uncle Philbert, and vanished.

"I'll get the chickens," added Aunt Mattie. But instead of leaving, she waded forward into one of the fragrant white drifts, a look of delight on her face. Bending over, she scooped up an armload of the fluffy stuff and let it cascade back to the floor. "It's so beautiful," she said. "Like a little blizzard." She gave Parker a smile. "I wonder if we could make snow angels?"

Ugh and Also Ew

The next morning the only sign of the Popcorn Incident was the presence of two odd-looking chickens, who were still chasing down a few remaining hard-to-reach kernels near the base of the stove. Aunt Mattie stepped around them as she lifted some kind of dough out of a deep fryer and placed it on newspaper laid out on the counter. An insanely delicious smell, combined with his gnawing hunger, had lured Parker out of bed at this unusually early hour. The deep fryer appeared to be the source of the wonderful smell. As he watched sleepily from the doorway of the kitchen, Aunt Mattie took a battered aluminum shaker and sifted powdered sugar onto the sizzling dough, then turned to greet him.

He braced himself for some reference to the Popcorn Incident, but Aunt Mattie simply asked him, "How does your corporosity seem to gashiate this morning?" Then, without waiting for an answer to this odd question, she added, "I got your favorite cereal, as requested." She indicated a large bowl of Bran Nuggets™ ("with wheat germ!"). Bran Nuggets™

("with wheat germ!") looked like gerbil food and tasted like cardboard, and Parker thought dark thoughts about his mother as he contemplated it. "Or," said Aunt Mattie quickly, "you could have some homemade doughnuts." She put a plate of them in front of him.

"And if that don't suit you," said Uncle Philbert from the other end of the table, where he was trying, and failing, to read a newspaper, "we got a little popcorn." He raised his eyebrows and indicated three trash cans and two large buckets in the corner, filled to the brim with the stuff. And that was the only time anyone referred to last night's events, except for Runcible. Every few minutes all morning long, the parrot made a noise *exactly* like a kernel of popcorn exploding, causing everyone to jump.

Uncle Philbert went back to trying to read the paper, but between spilling his coffee on it every time Runcible went "Pop" and chasing off a scrawny cat who kept draping himself over the exact section he was reading, he was having a tough time of it. Whenever he tried to outmaneuver the cat by starting a different section, the cat moved and planted himself on that same section, gazing lovingly up at Uncle Philbert and purring, as Uncle Philbert put it, "like a pastry." Parker felt it was too early in the morning, and probably not worth the effort, to point out to his great-uncle that pastries didn't purr.

But pastries—at least Aunt Mattie's homemade ones—*did* taste good. Parker was on his third doughnut when Uncle Philbert gave up the battle over the newspaper and stood, saying, "We got lots to do today, son. Chores first, of course. And then I'm goin' to teach you how to fish. Let's get a move on."

"Say please," said Runcible, in a perfect imitation of Aunt Mattie's voice.

"Please," said Uncle Philbert, without thinking, then looked peeved.

Aunt Mattie beamed. "Very good, Runcible," she cooed to the bird. To Parker she explained, "I'm trying to teach Runcible some manners. Her first owner was a sailor on a tramp steamer, and he taught her the *rudest* things. But the lessons seem to be rubbing off on Philbert as well. Right, dear?"

Uncle Philbert just harrumphed grumpily and picked up a bucket of popcorn and the bucket of food scraps from under the sink.

"Say thank you," Runcible said, and then added, in a voice that didn't sound at all like Aunt Mattie's, "you dish-faced moron."

Chores were bad enough, but fishing? Ugh. How much do I have to humor the old man? Parker wondered, trudging as slowly as possible after Uncle Philbert. He had little time to ponder this, however, for the moment they walked outside, a shiny silver BMW pulled up to the house and stopped beside them in a cloud of dust. The car's front door opened, and a large man unwedged himself from the leather driver's seat.

"Philbert Maxwell?" He was coming at them, right hand outstretched, left hand clutching a briefcase, face beaming. "I'm Franklin T. Numitz. Of Numitz Bilkum & Smattering. And this is your lucky day!"

Parker's first thought was that his great-uncle had won the lottery. He was sure that's how they delivered the news—in person, grinning from ear to ear, driving a sweet, late-model Beemer.

Uncle Philbert looked at the outstretched hand as if he were being offered a dead fish. He put down the two buckets he was holding but made no move to shake hands.

Mr. Numitz continued, apparently unfazed. "Mr. Maxwell," he repeated, grabbing Uncle Philbert's hand and pumping it up and down. "May I call you Phil? I'm so glad to have made your acquaintance at last. Do you mind if we go inside out of the sun and have a little talk?" He pulled a white handkerchief out of his suit pocket and wiped his forehead, then furtively cleaned his right hand. Perhaps he had noticed that Philbert's hand, the one he'd just shaken, had been carrying a pail of pig slops.

Uncle Philbert was just standing, looking at Mr. Numitz and saying nothing. *Kind of rude*, thought Parker. But then, that was Uncle Philbert for you. Not big on small talk.

At last he spoke. "No. You haven't. And I do," he said.

"Huh?"

"*No*, you can't call me Phil. *You haven't* made my acquaintance yet. And *I do* mind going inside. Got to feed the animals. And animals don't wait. *You* can wait, though, if you are so inclined."

"Oh. Um. Well. When will you be back?"

"When we're done feedin' the animals."

"When will that be?"

"When we're finished."

"I'll, um, wait on the porch, then."

"You do that."

Inside, the barn was cool and dark. In a pen at one end was a giant white pig covered in mud. On one side, the white horse was chewing on the door to his stall. Three really weird animals—they looked like half sheep, half camel—eyed Parker suspiciously; one of them drew back his lips and lobbed a gob of spit that just missed him. Everywhere were chickens and cats—dozens of cats—roaming or sitting in the shafts of soft speckled sunlight.

"How many cats do you have?" asked Parker, trying to count while he edged away from the strange-looking animals.

Uncle Philbert paused and thought for a moment. "Fourteen," he said. "No. Seventeen. No, twelve. Hard to keep track. Let's see. That's B. Bobbin Badcat there, and Johnny B. Goodcat. His sister Priscilla B. Goodcat. Then there are the Cat cats: That there's Cat Astrophe —has destroyed every piece of furniture we own. The black one's Cat Atonic—sleeps all day and all night, useless animal. You! Go catch a mouse! Cat Erwaul— howls all day and all night. Twin sisters Cat Alog and Cat Alump—just sit around like lumps on a log. Cat Erpillar—got seven toes on each paw. That orange one is Cat Sup. Over there's Cat Choo—she has dust allergies, sneezes all day long. Kat Mandu—he loves to climb. The chocolate one is Kit Kat. That tiny white one is Fat Cat. The runty striped one's Fraidy Cat. Scared of his own shadow." Parker recognized that one as the cat who'd been sitting on Uncle Philbert's newspaper. "And lastly Cat Cat. I think we'd run out of names by the time we got her. Seems every time I turn around your great-aunt has brought home another critter." He scooped up Fraidy Cat, who promptly started purring loudly and rubbing his head under Uncle Philbert's chin.

"A waste of space, each one," he grumbled. He made a broad gesture that included the whole barn. "Chickens too old to lay eggs. Motherless lambs. A horse too decrepit to ride. Goats that are just pains in the butt. Peacocks who preen all day long. A parrot who cusses at us. Bad-tempered, hay-burning llamas." So that's what the sheep-camels were. Llamas. "Useless varmints. All of you."

"What about the pig? He seems kinda useful."

"Useful? We get to feed him. But do we get to eat him? No, sir."

"Why not?"

"Because Matilda named him Oswald."

"So?"

"So you can't eat anything with a name."

Parker thought about that. "Yeah," he agreed. "It would be kinda weird to say, 'Would you like another slice of Oswald?' "

"Yes, indeed. Well, enough palaver. You go feed Oswald and the chickens. I'm going to feed the llamas." He handed Parker the two buckets and walked off. Parker was glad he didn't have to get near the llamas, but given his druthers, Parker realized he would "druther" not have to feed anyone—like the huge dirty pig or the harebrained chickens.

"Hey," he called after his great-uncle. "I thought we were going fishing?"

"When we're done," promised Uncle Philbert, who was approaching the llamas with a bucket of grain and a firm stare. "Mr. Rude," he said, running a hand along the neck of the meanest-looking one. "Mind your manners! Mr. Crude"—they were all crowding in on him now—"don't even think about biting me. Mr. Ugly, wait your turn!" The llamas might in fact have been bad-tempered, but what Aunt Mattie had said was true: they quickly gentled under Uncle Philbert's magic touch.

"Don't you have any"—what did they call those guys who work on farms?—"*hired hands* to do this work?"

Uncle Philbert nodded thoughtfully, as if the idea had just occurred to him. "I had a hired hand once. He was one gormy cuss. Numb as a pounded thumb and thick as marsh mud. And slow? He didn't move no better than a toad in a tar bucket. Why, he'd fummydiddle and fub around at some jeezly little job, sandpapering the anchor all day long. When all was said and done, why, the way he worked was no better than shearin' a pig: a great deal of noise and very little wool to show for it. No, he was a true hole in the snow, he was. Does that answer your question?"

Parker had the feeling his great-uncle had been speaking English, but he hadn't understood a single word. "So . . . that would be a no, then?" he said.

Uncle Philbert didn't seem to hear him, for at that moment one of the llamas nudged him in the face in an apparent effort to remind him that he hadn't fed them yet. Parker sighed and set to work. He managed to scatter the popcorn for the chickens and even to pour the food scraps into Oswald's trough without spilling too much on himself. At last he wiped his hands on his pants and went to find his great-uncle. Philbert was feeding Sugar—the swaybacked white nag from the veranda—and taking his time filling water troughs and grain bins. He seemed in no particular hurry.

"About this fishing thing," Parker asked, watching him work. "We don't have to dig for the worms, do we?"

Uncle Philbert snorted. "Worms? No! Any sand-for-brains can hang a worm on a hook and dangle it in the water."

Parker was a little surprised—and greatly relieved—to hear that. The idea of threading live worms onto hooks appealed to him about as much as the idea of eating them. "What are we going to use, then?"

"Flies, of course."

"We have to catch *flies*?"

Uncle Philbert laughed. "No, son. We have to *make* flies. We're going trout fishin', and no self-respectin' trout would look twice at anything but the best hand-tied fly." He straightened up. "Well, I've fubbed around here as long as I can. Best get goin'." He glanced out the barn door. "With any luck Mr. Dinglefuzzie will have given up and gone home by now."

Parker frowned. Suddenly he remembered: the Beemer guy.

"Why do you want him to leave? Isn't he going to tell you that you won some sort of prize? The lottery or something?"

Uncle Philbert snorted. "I seriously misdoubt it."

"Why is he here, then?"

Uncle Philbert removed his baseball cap and wiped some sweat from his forehead. "I suspect he's here," he said, "to try to take my farm away from me."

AKA Dinglefuzzie

Mr. Dinglefuzzie (known to the rest of the world as Mr. Numitz) was sitting in the kitchen, fanning himself with his hat and talking on the phone. According to Aunt Mattie, he had wandered the yard for a half hour trying in vain to use his cell phone. He had then asked if he could use their house phone to call his office. Mattie had produced the same funny phone Parker had tried to use and plugged it into a wall socket that Parker had somehow overlooked.

"Run it up the flagpole and see who salutes," Mr. Numitz was saying into the receiver as Uncle Philbert and Parker walked into the kitchen. "Float a trial balloon. See if that dog will hunt. And let's make sure we're all on the same page, financial-wise."

Parker gave Aunt Mattie a quizzical look. What on earth was Mr. Numitz talking about?

"Hunting hot-air balloons with dogs who, um . . . who salute," said Aunt Mattie in a whisper. "He's been talking like that nonstop. Do you think he has heat-stroke?"

"Do that ASAP," Mr. Numitz barked into the phone,

having caught sight of Philbert. "Gotta run." He hung up and turned with a broad smile. "Phil. That is, Philbert. Good to see you again."

Uncle Philbert just rolled his eyes and sat down at the kitchen table. Aunt Mattie produced a large pitcher of ice water and a few glasses. "Would you like something to drink, Mr. Numitz?"

Mr. Numitz mopped his brow with his handkerchief again. "Love some," he said. He frowned at the pitcher. "Got any sparkling water?"

Aunt Mattie gave him a questioning look.

"No? Never mind. I've got some here." He snapped open his briefcase, pulled out a bottle of clear liquid, and poured some into a glass. After watching it fizz for a moment, he drank it down.

Uncle Philbert picked up the bottle, sniffed it, and looked at the label. " 'Sportade Personal Rehydration System,' " he read aloud. "What's that?"

"Water," said Mr. Numitz, swallowing happily.

"And you pay"—Uncle Philbert glanced at the label again—"two dollars and ten cents for that?"

"Yessir."

Uncle Philbert shook his head. "Comes out of the tap for free, did you know that?"

Mr. Numitz clapped him on the shoulder. "Ha! Ha! *Love* your sense of humor! Well, now, Phil, let's talk turkey, if we may. As I said, this is your lucky day." He reached into his briefcase.

Awesome, thought Parker, who was still convinced the visitor was from the state lottery commission. Now was the moment when he would produce one of those humongous checks with the Maxwells' name on it.

Just then the phone rang, and everyone jumped at the unexpected noise. Mr. Numitz stopped talking and gave Aunt Mattie and Uncle Philbert a dismayed look, clearly waiting for them to answer it. Nobody made a move to do so, although Mr. Numitz looked like he was itching to go and pick it up. The phone continued to ring and ring. Finally Uncle Philbert gave a grunt of disgust, went over to the wall, and yanked the cord out of the socket.

"Er, Phil. Philbert. You do realize, do you not, that somebody was trying to reach you—or me—just then?" said Mr. Numitz.

"Young feller," said Uncle Philbert, "I had that phone installed for *my* convenience—not for the convenience of every Tom, Dick, and Alphonse out there. I plug it in when *I* need to use it. If Tom, Dick, or Alphonse wants to reach *me*, he can send a letter."

"Ah," said Mr. Numitz. "Well, that explains why we were never able to reach you by phone. Okay, then." He spread some papers out on the kitchen table. "Did you get our letters?"

"Yes."

"And?"

"They were very useful." Uncle Philbert gestured toward Runcible's empty cage. The floor of it was lined with white paper that looked suspiciously like business letters.

Mr. Numitz shook his head sadly. "Phil, you are

aware, are you not, that my client is prepared to offer you a *very* nice sum of money for your farm?"

He named an amount that made Parker's jaw drop. This was almost as good as winning the lottery. He turned to Uncle Philbert with wide eyes. Uncle Philbert appeared not to have heard.

"It's a very generous offer," Mr. Numitz continued, with the good-natured air of a game-show host bestowing vast riches on a contestant. "You could buy yourself a fine little condo in Florida with that money, yessirree. *And* have some left over for a couple of new cars, an RV, a boat. You just need to sign these Purchase and Sale agreements." He handed them to Uncle Philbert.

Parker's great-uncle took the papers and, without looking at them, walked over to the stove, opened the firebox, and shoved the papers in. They burst into flames as he closed the door with a loud clang.

"Does that answer your question?"

Mr. Numitz looked thunderstruck. Then he rose to his feet slowly. "Mr. Maxwell, Mrs. Maxwell, you need to know . . . you can't afford to . . ." He cleared his throat. "That turnpike exit ramp is going to go through your farm whether you want it to or not. The permits are all in order. Your neighbor has signed the agreement. You're the only holdout. I highly recommend that you reconsider your answer, because if you don't you'll be served—"

He was interrupted by the sound of Parker's cell phone ringing. It was the "Pop Goes the Weasel" ring tone, but every time it came to the part that said "Pop," it made a noise like popcorn exploding. Parker pulled it out and looked at it. How could it ring when there was no signal?

"You'll be served with—" Mr. Numitz tried to continue, but once again he was interrupted by a phone ringing. This time it was the Maxwells' old phone. Parker picked up the phone cord and looked at the end of it. It wasn't plugged in. What the heck was going on?

"I reckon that's for me," said Uncle Philbert, giving Parker a secret wink and reaching for the phone. "Good day, Mr. . . . Dinglefuzzie."

Mr. Numitz did not appear to take the hint. As he opened his mouth to speak one more time, he was stopped by the sound of a cell phone's jarring ring. He pulled his own phone out of his pocket and flicked it open. "It's ringing," he said in confusion, "but there's no signal." He punched a button. "Hello? Hello? Hello?"

"I'll just show Mr. Numitz to the door, shall I?" said Aunt Mattie. And when she returned, she looked sternly up at the ceiling, where a certain gray parrot clung upside down to the light fixture. "That's enough of *that*," she said firmly.

"Okey dokey," said Runcible, looking decidedly pleased with herself.

Storm Clouds

After breakfast the next day Uncle Philbert went to the defective-sports-equipment closet and pulled out a long, slender metal tube, a fishing net, and a strange-looking vest.

"Reach me down those hats, son," he said, indicating two baseball caps over the kitchen door. One was a Red Sox cap. Parker stuck that one on his head. The other had some odd writing on it. He passed that one to his great-uncle.

"What's *Illegitimi non carborundum*?" he asked.

Uncle Philbert turned that hat over and looked at the saying embroidered on it. "That's my motto." When he saw Parker's blank look, he sighed. "These modern schools. Don't they teach Latin anymore?"

Parker doubted it was worth mentioning that he'd taken Latin for one whole year. Seeing as how he'd gotten a D+ in it, and all.

"It means 'Don't let the—' "

" '—turkeys,' " inserted Aunt Mattie.

" '—get you down,' " Uncle Philbert finished. "Sort

of. Come on," he added, heading for the door and passing Parker a wicker backpack that Aunt Mattie had been filling with food. "You can carry lunch. Let's go ketch us some fish."

"Where are we going?" Parker asked. Uncle Philbert nodded toward a distant tree-covered hill, topped with a water tower and a solitary house, on the far side of a vast rolling pasture. Parker sighed heavily and headed toward the car. Uncle Philbert stopped him.

"Can't drive there."

"How do we get there, then?"

"Gotta walk."

"*Walk?*"

"Yep." He opened the gate to the pasture for his great-nephew.

Parker gaped. "But that's a hundred miles away. No way. I can't walk that far."

"Suit yourself," said Philbert. "Hand me the food."

Parker shrugged the backpack off his back and started to hand it to his uncle. A delicious odor was drifting from the top of it—something chocolatey and cinnamony and warm from the oven. As usual, his stomach was frantic. He had polished off all the snacks he'd brought in just one day, and even though it had only been a short while since breakfast, he was hungry. After a moment of hesitation, he slung the basket on his back again.

"All right," he muttered. "I'll come." He followed his great-uncle through the gate into the pasture and glanced at the impossibly distant hillside. Camp Cramalama suddenly seemed like it might not have been such a bad idea. He was sure computer geeks weren't made to go on hundred-mile hikes.

It took them over an hour to reach the ridge, the hot sun beating on their shoulders. Uncle Philbert seemed lost in thought, and Parker didn't say much. He was grateful for the silence—he hated having to make small talk with grown-ups.

Uncle Philbert stopped from time to time to push a fence rail back into place, or pull up a thistle that was sprouting in the pasture, or let Parker rest. Pausing at a gate while Parker caught his breath, he turned his gaze to his great-nephew and announced, "Built this whole fence myself when I was a young man. Took me all summer. Me and the hired hand."

"You lived here all your life?" This was an amazing notion to Parker, who had already lived in four different houses in two different towns.

"Uh-huh. Started off with fifty acres and built it up to this." His gesture took in the sweep of the horizon. "Now, dang it! See what I mean about that hired hand? Everything he built came out weewaw. This gate ain't never worked right." He had to haul hard on the gate to lift it out of its lock and let Parker step through. "You want it done right, you got to do it yourself."

"Is this the same fence you built?"

"Pretty much. Wood's a bit dozey in places, and these ding-busted gates are all crooked, but it's still horse high, bull strong, and hog tight."

"What's that mean?"

"Means it's *high* enough to keep a horse from jumping over it, *strong* enough to keep a bull from knockin' it down, and *tight* enough to keep a hog from squeezin' through it. Now, here we are."

They were, at last, at the foot of the steep wooded ridge. Here a rocky stream emerged from the trees and cascaded in a kind of waterfall down a broad, flat rockface into a deep pool—almost wide enough to be a small pond—before thinning back into a stream and dipping out of sight around the bottom of the pasture. They crossed the downstream end of the pool and headed toward the shade of the trees. Uncle Philbert sat heavily on a boulder in the shade while Parker shrugged off the backpack and stretched out on the mossy bank of the pool. It felt blissful to get out of the sun. Even the bugs seemed too worn out by the heat to bother buzzing around them.

From where he lay on his back, Parker had a good view of the water tower on the ridgetop, the tower that had seemed so far away only an hour ago. Up close, it looked like a squat rocket ship balanced on six long legs. A metal ladder ran up one leg all the way to the very top. Philbert followed his gaze.

"Now, when I was a young feller, we used to dare each other to climb that water tower," he said, passing Parker a thermos full of a cold blue liquid. "It's the tallest thing for miles around. Great view, if you can stomach heights."

"You *climbed* that?"

"Scared the bejeezus out of me."

Parker was impressed. He had no stomach for

heights. He didn't have a head for heights either. Or the legs or arms or any other thing that heights seemed to require. His mind immediately, inevitably, went back to that day on top of the Empire State Building. It had been so special. His tenth birthday, just him and his father. Lunch at the Ritz in New York. A slight detour while Dad made a visit to the fancy marble-lined offices of one of his biggest clients. Further delay while Parker had to shake hands with men in suits and hear what a great guy his father was, what a fantastic lawyer, and yada yada boringcakes.

It seemed to take forever, but at last, there they were at the Empire State Building. Because, what was a visit to New York if you didn't climb the Empire State Building and test to see if you dropped a penny off the observation deck would it really go straight through a car parked on the street, like everybody said.

By the time the elevator doors finally opened at the top floor, Dad had gotten caught up in Parker's excitement. Together they darted out the elevator to the windows to take in the sight of New York City, spread out a thousand feet below. And that's when things started to go pear-shaped for Parker. Though he was safely indoors, he suddenly found he had to keep one trembling hand pressed against a solid wall at all times just to bring himself to look out the floor-to-ceiling windows. His head swam, his heart pounded, his knees felt spongy, and his breath came in painful spurts. His father, oblivious to Parker's distress, grabbed the door to the outside observation deck and flung it open, grinning.

"Are you coming, buddy?" Dad's words were slightly muffled by the wind as he held the door open.

"Sure. Yeah. Just a minute."

When his fingers closed over the asthma inhaler in his pocket, Parker realized it would be easy to claim he couldn't go out that door—outdoors!—onto the open-air observation deck because he was having an asthma attack.

"Come on. The view's awesome."

"Sorry, Dad," he gasped. "Sorry. I can't." Then he had faked taking a drag on the inhaler.

Dad had hidden his disappointment well, Parker was forced to admit. Maybe that was because he had so much practice at hiding disappointment. Disappointment that Parker wasn't brave. Or smart, or popular, or athletic, or any of those things that make a father proud to be the father of you, instead of the father of someone like, say, his cousin Simon. His dad could have pointed out to Parker that the deck was perfectly safe—walled in with a high fence. He could have pointed out the young children who were unafraid to go out on it. Or the little old ladies clinging to their headscarves in the wind. He could have pointed all that out, but he didn't need to. Parker could see it for himself. It made no difference. He couldn't have walked through that door if his life had depended on it.

"Are you coming, son?"

"Huh?"

"I said, time for a swim. Are you coming?" His great-uncle had donned some sort of ancient bathing trunks and was looking at Parker expectantly.

"What about fishing?"

"Too hot. Days like this, even the fish take the afternoon off and go swimming."

So Parker peeled off his T-shirt and, wearing only his shorts, dove in. The icy water felt wonderful on his sweaty back, his sore leg muscles. He swam around lazily until he actually felt cold. When he got out, Uncle Philbert had spread the food and some fly-tying gear out on a blanket. Along with a dozen chocolate cinnamon cookies and the thermos of what turned out to be blueberry lemonade, Aunt Mattie had packed sandwiches wrapped in wax paper and a half dozen small, spotted hard-boiled eggs. Parker held one up and looked at his great-uncle.

"Come from guinea hens," said Uncle Philbert. "Only critters on the farm that are good for *anything*."

While Parker devoured his share of the picnic, Uncle Philbert busied himself tying a wisp of yellow fluff to a hook whose point was set in the toe of his work boot. He plucked the hook out of the boot and held up the half-finished fly for Parker to admire.

"Duckling down," he said. "I call it the Yellow Terror. You ready to try casting?" He pulled a flannel cloth out of the metal tube and unwrapped it. Inside were two slender, tapering octagonal segments of bamboo. The fatter piece had a reel at one end. Uncle Philbert snapped the two sections together, threaded some fishing line from the reel down the length of the rod, and passed the contraption to Parker.

He was surprised at how light the rod was—and disappointed to find that the fishing line ended in a bare hook.

"Where's my fly?" he demanded.

"Try this." Uncle Philbert pushed a tiny bit of cork onto the end of the hook.

"I'm not going to catch anything with a *cork*."

"Darn right. I got no interest in havin' you take my eyeballs out. Let's go stand in that clearing. I'll give you a lesson. Hand me the rod."

Watching Uncle Philbert demonstrate, Parker could see that fly casting was like cracking a really long horsewhip. While the rod in your right hand kept the tip of the whip—the fishhook—zipping back and forth overhead, your left hand had to pull more and more line out of the reel so that the whip got longer and longer. And then, just at the exact right moment—*zap!*—you flicked the whole rod straight ahead, released the extra line in your left hand, and let the fly shoot forward and settle gently in the exact spot you aimed at. That was the idea, anyway.

It was amazing to watch Uncle Philbert. He stood holding the fly rod loosely, right elbow tucked in to his side, the rest of his arm hardly moving as he whipped longer and longer strands of fish line back and forth in the air, like a cowboy with a graceful lariat. Then, with a barely noticeable flick of his wrist, he would let it all fly. He could land that hook within inches of the baseball cap he'd set as a target thirty yards away on the ground.

"Easy as eatin' pie," said Uncle Philbert. A complete

lie, as Parker discovered when Uncle Philbert passed the rod to him. Unless, of course, eating pie was horribly complicated and involved catching a fishhook in your hair. And your clothes. And your great-uncle. Parker's first attempts to cast were miserable failures. He quickly saw why Uncle Philbert had covered the hook in cork, and why he was made to practice in the clearing instead of by the pool, where the hook would have ended up in the overhanging tree branches.

After an hour of coaching him, and after extracting a hook that had somehow managed to snag the picnic basket, Uncle Philbert took the rod back and said he was going to make a few casts into the water. First he replaced Parker's naked hook with the finished Yellow Terror.

"Why don't you just use one of those?" Parker pointed to the row of oddly colored flies stuck into the brim of the *Illegitimi* baseball cap.

"That won't do. Not if you want to catch the Old Baister. He's too smart."

"What's the Old Baister?"

"Great big brown trout. Who knows how old he is? I been fishin' for him for years. Hooked him seven times. Landed him three times, and he got away four times."

"How can you catch the same fish seven times?"

Uncle Philbert reached over with a pair of pliers from the tackle box and flattened the barb of the Yellow Terror's hook. "It's called ketch and release." He stood up and started his cast. "You don't use a barbed hook, so you can release the fish soon as you ketch it. No harm done. It's kind of a game between us now. I've

65

caught this feller so many times, I know what he looks
like. He's got a little circular scar on his tail and a big
nick out of his dorsal fin."

As he spoke, Uncle Philbert released the line and the
Yellow Terror flew across the water and settled lightly
near a big boulder that poked out of the water on the
far, shady side of the pool. "That's his favorite spot
there." Uncle Philbert let the fly float downstream

away from the boulder. Nothing. With his left hand he pulled the line back until he could lift the fly out of the water and start a new cast. Two, three, four times he cast, each time pulling the empty line back in. After what must have been a dozen tries, there was a flash in the water and a large fish shot headfirst from the pool. He arched into the air, gleaming dark and shiny in the sun for an instant before falling back with a loud splash that created a broad round ripple.

"You got him!" Parker shouted. Then he noticed that the Yellow Terror was floating untouched on the surface.

Uncle Philbert laughed and reeled the fly back in.

"What are you doing? You almost had him," said Parker as Uncle Philbert began packing the rod away. "That was him, wasn't it? The Old Baister?"

"Oh, yes, I reckon. But he's just playin' with me. Laughin' at me. Come on. Time to be gettin' home."

"But we didn't catch anything."

"There's always next time."

"Wait. Let me get this straight," said Parker, flabbergasted. "We walked a million miles so I could cast in a *field*?"

"Next time you can try castin' in the stream. You're a quick study there."

That shut Parker up for a moment. Nobody had called him a quick study at *anything* before. Ever.

"But I was just getting the hang of it. Couldn't we—"

"We're gonna get a duckin' if we don't hightail it home. Rain's coming."

"How can you tell?" The sky was blue, and the nearest clouds were on the far horizon. It couldn't have looked less like rain to Parker. Uncle Philbert cocked an eye toward the sky, sniffed the air like some sort of hunting dog, and settled his cap on his head.

"Weather's changing. Wind's backing into the northeast. Besides, it just smells like rain, don't it?"

It didn't smell like rain to Parker. It smelled like hot summer day. It smelled like peanut butter sandwiches, damp bathing suits, and laziness, with just a hint of wood smoke mixed in. He shrugged. Maybe you had to be a farmer to know what about-to-rain smells like. Shouldering the picnic basket, he hurried to catch up with Uncle Philbert.

"Now then, young whiffet, at that highfalutin school you go to—the one where they don't teach you Latin—do they teach you how to speak Ob?"

"Ob? Never heard of it."

"Well, as Mark Twain once said, Never let your schoolin' interfere with your education. It's time you got a proper education. Ob is real easy. You just stick an *ob* in the middle of each syllable of every word. Like this: Yes is y*ob*es. No is n*ob*o. Dish-faced moron is . . ."

Fly Away Home

The storm must have been coming even faster than Uncle Philbert predicted, because he seemed to have picked up the pace. After a few minutes Parker was having trouble keeping up. He stopped practicing Ob in his head long enough to feel around for his inhaler. With a sick feeling, he discovered it wasn't in its pocket. He remembered he had left it back by the pool, on the big boulder. Telling Uncle Philbert to wait for him, he jogged back to the stream as fast as he could. By the time he got there, he was panting for breath. It was a scary feeling for Parker to be breathless and not have his inhaler close at hand. He headed for the boulder, then stopped short. The inhaler was gone. Two boys were sitting beside the pool, next to the boulder, tossing stones into the water. Parked behind them were two lime green ATVs.

The bigger of the two boys stood up, gripping the waistband of his jeans in one hand to keep them from sliding off.

"Who are you?" he asked Parker, as he settled a baseball cap backward on his head.

"I'm . . ." began Parker, then stopped. Why were *they* grilling *him*? This was Uncle Philbert's land. "This is my great-uncle's property," he said, trying hard not to wheeze. "Who are *you*?"

"So that whack-job is your great-uncle?" asked the boy, snickering. "And I bet this is yours." From his pocket he pulled Parker's inhaler.

Craptastic! thought Parker, but he said nothing, since he couldn't trust his voice to be steady. He approached the boy slowly, willing his heart and breathing to slow down, trying to convince himself that the shortness of breath was not an asthma attack. *I'm just out of breath from running. I'm fine. I don't really need that inhaler. I just—*

The boy held up the inhaler, but instead of tossing it to Parker he pressed the button on the top, releasing a little spray of lifesaving mist into the breeze. Parker froze. The boy pressed it a second time, and a third. If he kept it up, the inhaler would soon be empty. The very thought made Parker's heart start racing again. The boy wasn't even looking at him—he was looking at his friend and laughing—but he was still too far away for Parker to make a grab for the inhaler.

"Hey," said the boy, switching his gaze back to Parker, "has your uncle changed his mind about the turnpike deal yet?"

"No. And how do you know about that?" Parker was disgusted to hear the tremor in his voice.

"My father says he'll sign it, if he knows what's good for him." The laugh was gone, and there was no mistaking the menace in the boy's voice. "I have this funny feeling your great-uncle's about to change his mind."

"What are you talking about?" asked Parker.

"You'll find out soon enough," the boy said with a snicker. "So you want this back?" He held out the inhaler and took a few steps in Parker's direction.

"Yes," said Parker, but his voice cracked. *I am such a sissy.*

"Okay," said the boy. "Catch." And as Parker held out his hands, the boy tossed the inhaler in a lazy high loop far over his head. Parker watched in dismay as it splashed into the middle of the pool. "Oops.

Sorry," said the boy. "Guess you'll have to play Go Fish."

He turned and headed for the ATVs, his friend following close behind. Parker dashed into the water, not even bothering to remove his shoes, trying frantically to locate the inhaler. But he couldn't tell exactly where it had landed. He heard the boys start their engines as he cast about in thigh-deep water.

"Here's a message for your great-uncle," the older boy called back to him as he revved his engine. "He should make like a ladybug and fly away home." Then, laughing at their own joke, the two boys kicked their ATVs into gear and headed up the ridge, spraying dirt and gouging ruts into the soft soil.

He should tell Uncle Philbert what had happened at the stream—after all, it involved him as well as Parker. But it was all too humiliating. He was such a coward. If he told, that would make him a tattletale, too. Uncle Philbert would realize his great-nephew was both a chicken and a rat. He was wondering whether such an animal existed—the chicken-rat—and still hurrying to catch up with his great-uncle when he turned a corner in the path and nearly ran right into him. The old man was standing stock-still. Just standing, and staring.

"What . . . ?" Parker began. He glanced at the advancing clouds. Was it about to storm? Then he saw where his uncle was looking. Not up, but down. He was looking at the distant hay field that sloped down to his rambling red farmhouse and barn.

The field was on fire. And the fire was heading straight for the Maxwells' house.

Missing Mattie

At the top of the field—the field of crisp dry stubble baking in the July sun—someone had built a bonfire. They had built the fire out of fence railings, and those railings looked suspiciously like Uncle Philbert's fence railings. Worse, the fire had somehow spread to the surrounding field.

The wind was driving the fire downhill toward the farmhouse, scorching the field black as it went. As Parker watched, horrified, little tongues of red flame licked at the far edge of the scorch mark and curls of white smoke rose up to meet the approaching clouds.

"We've got to get help," he said frantically. "Call the fire department—before it gets to the house, and the barn."

But Uncle Philbert didn't budge. What was wrong with the old man? This was urgent. To Parker's astonishment, Uncle Philbert just laughed. He stood there rubbing a hand over the crisp, dry stubble of his unshaven chin, and shook his head and laughed.

"No need to bother," he said, and when Parker

looked at him in utter confusion, he merely jerked his chin at the sky. "Wind's about to change."

Parker could see nothing in the sky to back up this claim, but when he looked back at the field he began to see what his great-uncle meant. The breeze fanning the fire was dying down. For a moment it stopped altogether. The flames paused briefly. When the wind sprang up again moments later, it was blowing much harder, and from the opposite direction. The advancing fire changed its course, like an army whose general has abruptly altered his battle plan and sounded retreat. The flames swerved off to the left and then began racing back up the hill toward the ridge, the wind at their back whipping them on.

Uncle Philbert gave a rueful laugh as he watched where the fire was heading. Directly in its new path was the solitary house carved into the woods at the top of the ridge, a house with two green ATVs parked in front.

"Someone's gonna get a nasty shock," Uncle Philbert said. He looked at the remains of his fence railings, smoldering in the center of the blackened field, then held out a hand to catch a single drop of rain. "For a few minutes, anyway," he added. "Come on, son. Let's get home."

By the time they arrived back at the farmhouse twenty minutes later, those first drops of rain had turned into a steady downpour. They ducked into the kitchen, and Parker looked around in surprise. Aunt Mattie was nowhere to be seen. He was sure she would have been right there waiting for them, eager for details about the fire. Uncle Philbert looked equally surprised.

"Matilda!" he called. There was no answer.

A half-peeled potato rested on the kitchen counter, next to a half-frosted cake. From the warming oven came the smell of roasting chicken. But Aunt Mattie was neither in the kitchen nor—after a thorough search—in any other part of the house or the barn.

Parker and Uncle Philbert made their way back into the kitchen and stood there, their rain-soaked clothes dripping onto the tiled floor.

"Maybe she went on an errand," suggested Parker finally.

Uncle Philbert shook his head. "Car's in the drive-way," he said.

Parker inspected the half-finished cake. "It's like she was abducted by aliens right in the middle of making dinner."

"I'm completely flummoxed," Uncle Philbert admitted, sitting down at the kitchen table. That's when Parker noticed the piece of paper, in the center of the table, held in place by a large apple. He picked it up, read it, and passed it to Uncle Philbert.

Bertie, dear, said the note, in Aunt Mattie's swirly handwriting. *Supper's in the oven. Don't wait on me to eat. I've been arrested.*

"Arrested!" Uncle Philbert sighed, then sank into a chair. "Holy hijinks, woman. What have you gone and done now?" He drummed his fingers on the kitchen table and reread the note. Parker was baffled by his great-uncle's reaction.

"Come on," Parker cried, jumping to his feet. "Don't just sit there. We've got to go rescue Aunt Matilda."

Uncle Philbert gave him a skeptical look. "And just how are you planning on doin' that?"

Parker wasn't sure. But something Uncle Philbert had just said gave him an inspiration. He squared his shoulders and raised his index finger.

"To the Batmobile!" he said.

Shut Up and . . . Whatever

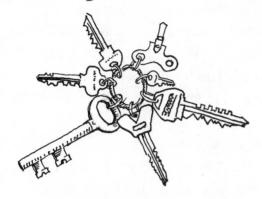

"Uncle Philbert, do you even *know* how to drive?"

The two of them were in the front seat of the black 1946 taxicab that served as the Maxwells' car.

"Of course," snapped Uncle Philbert. "What do you take me for, some kind of nincompoop?"

Parker said nothing. So far, Uncle Philbert had tried to start the car with an enormous key that looked like it might open the door of a seventeenth-century castle, the kind inhabited by vampires. Next he'd tried a tiny key that clearly went to a girl's diary, followed by the key that wound the grandfather clock in the living room. Parker watched as his great-uncle frowned, picked yet another key off the big round key ring, and inspected it closely.

"That one goes to the chest in the hallway," said Parker, trying hard to keep the impatience out of his voice. "The one with all the Batman comics." At this rate they would never get to the police station in time to save Aunt Mattie. He wasn't quite sure *what* they were saving her from. A dank and windowless dungeon infested by rats, perhaps. Something dire, at any rate.

"I knew that," said Uncle Philbert, who had clearly been about to try to insert it into the ignition.

"Try this one." Parker reached over and plucked the only key off the ring that could possibly start a car.

"Hmmph," grumped Uncle Philbert. "I was just about to pick that one." He leaned over and aimed the key at the ignition.

At last, breathed Parker to himself. But Uncle Philbert had frozen, the key a hairbreadth away from the ignition. After a moment, he let his hand drop.

"What's wrong? I'm sure that's the right key."

The old man chewed on his mustache, a sheepish look spreading over his face.

Parker groaned. "You *don't* know how to drive, do you?" Another thought struck him. "Do you even have a driver's license?"

"I did, once. When I was a boy, you could get your license at twelve, if you lived on a farm. But it might have expired. Do those things expire? Because—"

Parker grabbed his great-uncle's wrist. "Shut up and drive, Uncle Philbert," he said. *"Please."*

"Yes, well, see . . . The problem is, Matilda never lets me drive the car because I . . . sometimes I have this bad effect on machines. Just sometimes, mind you," he added hastily. "But Matilda is awful fond of this car. Rebuilt the engine herself from scratch. So I ain't never really actually tried to . . . And it would be a terrible shame if I was to . . ."

He trailed off, and Parker leaned his head back on the seat with a moan. He had a sudden image of all the broken machinery—the vacuum cleaner, the chain saw, the dishwasher, the lawn mower—that littered the property. He realized why it had not surprised him when Philbert's attempt to hook up the phone to call the police station had resulted in the complete destruction of the phone plug. Aunt Mattie's words echoed in his head: *He is death on machines . . . One touch from him . . .*

Parker looked over at Uncle Philbert. "Now what?"

"I don't reckon *you* know how to drive a car by any chance?" his great-uncle asked.

Parker started to shake his head, but then a sudden thought occurred to him. "Yes," he said, sitting up straight. "I do. I'm a pro." Well, it wasn't a complete lie. He'd made it to the "Pro" level just the other day, driving his souped-up Porsche, playing Indy 500. Of course, that hadn't ended very well, but he couldn't think about that now. Aunt Mattie needed them. "Shove over, Uncle Philbert," he said, and slid into the driver's seat.

The key fit the ignition perfectly. He paused, his fingers trembling a bit. Uncle Philbert saw the hesitation. "Atomic batteries to power," he announced, grabbing the dashboard. "Turbines to speed."

Parker gave him a nervous smile. "Roger, Batman. Ready to move out."

He turned the key.

The engine purred into life, and the car lurched forward across the barnyard. He was doing it! He was driving! It was just like Indy 500. Simple. Except . . . while he was great at steering, he wasn't too sure about the rest of it. All those confusing pedals, for example. He glanced down at them and—"Watch out for

Sugar!"—tried to remember which was the brake—
"Don't kill those chickens!"—and what that other one
was for. He swerved just in time to avoid a goat, looked
down at the pedals again, hit something with a thump,
and finally found the driveway. Philbert, he noticed,
had a white-knuckle grip on the dashboard. They
hadn't gotten very far down the driveway, creeping
along as fast as he could make the car go—a very un-
Indy-500 fifteen miles per hour—when Uncle Philbert
cleared his throat.

"You planning on shifting into second gear anytime
soon?"

"Second gear?" Indy 500 cars didn't have any second
gear. It was Parker's turn to look sheepish and Uncle
Philbert's turn to roll his eyes.

"I think you do something with this stick here." Uncle Philbert reached for the gearshift.

"Don't touch it!" cried Parker, but it was too late. The moment Uncle Philbert moved the lever, the engine gave an unearthly howl and the car shuddered to a halt.

Parker leaned his head back against the seat and sighed. "Game over," he muttered. Sugar gave him a baleful look from the safety of the veranda, and two guinea hens with ruffled feathers hopped onto the hood of the car and began marching about with the distinct air of shoppers looking for the Complaints Department.

Uncle Philbert was the first to break the silence. "Something tells me you don't have a real, actual license."

"Really? What gave it away?"

"Might have been the way you mistook the gas pedal for the brake," said Philbert thoughtfully.

"Or possibly the part where I mowed down the henhouse?" asked Parker.

"That, too," admitted Uncle Philbert.

"So it's probably a good thing the car died when it did," concluded Parker, remembering what happened in the Mean Streets Auto game when the cops caught you driving without a license. "We would have gone Directly to Jail. Without passing Go."

"Or collecting two hundred doll—" began Uncle Philbert. But Parker interrupted him midsentence.

"Wait a minute!" he exclaimed. "That's it! I've got it!"

"What?"

"Yes, it's genius," he continued, talking to himself as much as to Uncle Philbert. "But how can we do it without a car?" He tapped his fingers impatiently against the steering wheel. There had to be a way. And there *was* a way. Forget Indy 500. Time for Triple Crown. "Sugar!" he shouted.

"You feelin' all right?" asked Uncle Philbert. "Hit your head on the dashboard?"

Parker smiled at him. "I don't reckon," he said, in a fair imitation of Uncle Philbert's voice, "you know how to ride a horse?"

"Come on," said Uncle Philbert. "This was your idea. And a dandy one at that."

That hadn't been Uncle Philbert's first reaction to Parker's plan. His first reaction had been to tell him he was nuts. That it would take days—no, weeks—to get to the police station by horse. And it was sure to be illegal. "I hope so," Parker had said at the time. Now as he stood there, frozen, one foot on the veranda, the other halfway over Sugar's broad back, Parker was having serious second thoughts. He was wishing Uncle Philbert had talked him out of this crazy idea.

"When I said 'ride,'" Parker tried to explain as he gripped the porch rail, "I meant *you*, not me. I'm kind of . . . allergic to horses." What he actually meant, what he'd forgotten in the excitement of the moment, was that he was *terrified* of horses. On the video screen they were fine. In person, or rather in animal, they were big and smelly and dirty and, well, *big*. "My doctor says—"

"So you're just going to stand there and let Aunt Matilda rot in jail?"

"No, of course not. I—"

"C'mon, then. Time's a wastin'. Can you ride a horse or not?"

Parker looked at Sugar, standing utterly still under Uncle Philbert's gentle touch, and drew a deep breath.

"Sure," he muttered. "I'm a pro." He closed his eyes and slid the rest of the way onto Sugar's back. "Roger. Ready to move out," he managed to say.

"Power to turbines," said Uncle Philbert, climbing on behind Parker and thrusting the reins into his great-nephew's hands. "Now shut up and drive."

You Have the Right

The double yellow line meant no passing—none at all, whatsoever. So by the time the police car finally arrived, its blue lights flashing, the line of cars jostling and honking angrily behind Sugar stretched far into the distance. It was like when the cars got stuck behind the school bus each morning, only worse.

The police officer was polite, infuriatingly polite. It took a great deal of hard work and every ounce of Uncle Philbert's patience to get himself arrested. Time and again the officer tried to convince Uncle Philbert that if he would just go home, riding on the shoulder of the road instead of smack down the middle, everyone would forget this ever happened.

"No, sir," insisted Uncle Philbert. "I got just as much right to use this road as any car. My tax dollars paid for this road. I intend to use it—every dad-blamed inch of it." He glared at the officer, a gangly young man whose straw-colored hair stuck up in tufts and whose bony wrists and ankles protruded from his uniform, giving him the air of a scarecrow whose clothes had been intended for a younger and smaller sibling.

The officer sighed. "In that case, I'm afraid I'm going to have to arrest you."

"High time you did, too," huffed Uncle Philbert.

After hunting through his pockets, the officer at last produced a note card and began reading Uncle Philbert his rights, peering closely at the paper.

"You have the right to an attorney—"

"What's the world comin' to when the police refuse to do their duty, I ask you," continued Philbert. "I mean to say, my taxes pay your salary and I expect you to do your job." He slid off Sugar's back and stuck out his wrists. "Cuff me! Take me in. Now then, Parker, you take Sugar home and—"

"You have the right to—"

"No way!" cried Parker, jumping down, too. "I'm not missing out on this. I deserve to be arrested, too."

Uncle Philbert tried to argue, but Parker insisted he couldn't ride a horse by himself. Uncle Philbert gave in and the two of them went to tie Sugar to a convenient tree, the policeman trotting close behind them.

". . . and you have the right to—" The policeman squinted at the card in the fading light, then showed it to Uncle Philbert. "I can't make out that word there, can you?"

Uncle Philbert held the card out at arm's length and tilted his head. *"Remain silage,"* he pronounced at last. "Or possibly *Remain silent.* Now can we get a move on? I ain't got all night."

"Thanks," said the cop. *"You have the right to remain silage . . ."*

Good luck with that one, Parker thought, sliding into the backseat of the police car.

No one seemed more relieved to see Uncle Philbert than the police officer in charge of Aunt Mattie's case. Sergeant Smith ushered the three of them into a room with a floor covered in linoleum the color of mustard— the cheerful yellow mustard of ballpark franks, that is, not the dingy brown mustard eaten by people who want you to think they drive about in expensive cars and employ a personal chef named Jean-Claude.

"Mr. Maxwell, sir, please be seated," said the sergeant. "I'm very happy to see you. We've been trying to reach you," he began, "but your phone seems to be out of order. We're hoping you could convince Mrs. Maxwell—"

"Um, sir," interrupted the other officer, whose name, Parker could see from his uniform, was Jones. "Mr. Maxwell isn't here about Mrs. Maxwell. He's here because he's under arrest, too. He insisted," he added unhappily.

Sergeant Smith's face fell. "Oh, lovely," he muttered. "Just what we need. Another Maxwell. What's *he* charged with?"

Officer Jones looked perplexed. "Um. Well. Operating a motor vehicle without a . . . without a . . ."

"Without a motor?" supplied Uncle Philbert helpfully. "It was a horse," he explained to the desk sergeant. Then his face took on a fierce expression. "And

86

now, you young whiffet, what exactly is all this folderol and flapdoodle about arresting Mrs. Maxwell?"

"We got a call from someone who said you were burning one of your fields and it got out of control," the sergeant began. "The caller said it was about to burn their house down. So we checked—"

"Who exactly called you?" asked Uncle Philbert.

"Er, it was an anonymous call," said the sergeant. "Lucky for you, the rain put the fire out, but it seems you never got a permit for burning your fields. So we—"

Parker jumped to his feet. "I demand to see my lawyer!" he said, with a dramatic flourish. It was not for nothing that he had watched hundreds of hours of cop shows on TV. Both men gave him a look, however, and he sat down again.

"We charged Mrs. Maxwell with burning without a permit, reckless endangerment of property, attempted arson—"

"You charged Matilda with arson?"

"Well . . ." The sergeant blushed to the tips of his ears. "We were just going to fine her. But she insisted on being arrested."

Uncle Philbert shook his head. "I heard of *resisting* arrest, but *insisting* on arrest?"

"Yes. We really just brought her in to ask her some questions, but she said"—he consulted a small note-book—"that there was a 'right and proper way to do things, and if a thing was to be done it must be done properly.' Perhaps we should go talk to her? She can explain." So he led them down a hallway to a holding

cell, where Aunt Matilda sat, knitting happily. The door to the cell, Parker couldn't help noticing, was ajar.

"Bertie, dear. And Parker. How kind of you to come visit me in the Big House. I see you've met Sergeant Smith. Now, Sergeant, dear, let me have your hands." The sergeant blushed again, looked around to see if anyone was watching, and thrust both hands through the bars of the cell. Aunt Mattie approached with her knitting, and for a wild moment Parker thought she meant to tie the policeman's hands together with yarn, binding them around the cell bars, so that she could make good her escape. Instead, she held out her knitting and measured it against his hands.

"Nearly done," she said, holding up a single mitten for Parker to admire. "Nothing passes the time like knitting," she explained. "When you're in the slammer, that is. And I thought I might as well start paying my debt to society, or at least to Sergeant Smith." She looked at Uncle Philbert. "Have you come to bust me out of here?"

"No," said Uncle Philbert. "I—"

"Good," said Aunt Mattie. "Because that won't be necessary. I've formulated a—" She broke off and glanced at Sergeant Smith. "Cover your ears, Sergeant, dear. This is confidential information." She lowered her voice. "I've got an escape plan." She reached into a pocket of her apron and pulled out a spoon, holding it triumphantly in front of her.

"What's that?" asked Parker.

Aunt Mattie gave him a disappointed look. "What

does it look like, dear heart? It's a spoon. I stole it off my supper tray."

"So?"

"So I can use it to tunnel out of here."

"But it's a spoon, Aunt Mattie. A *plastic* spoon."

"Well, it might take a while. But according to *Huckleberry Finn* and *The Count of Monte Cristo* and *The Great Escape*—"

"Aunt Mattie," said Parker with a sigh, "you read too many books. Way too many books."

"And you," said Aunt Mattie, "are a party pooper." She replaced the spoon in her pocket and looked over at Uncle Philbert. "Well, if you're not here to spring me from the pokey, what *are* you here for?"

"I'm under arrest, too," said Uncle Philbert. Then he explained the whole thing to Mattie and the sergeant: how he and Parker had discovered the bonfire, and the burning fields, and Aunt Mattie's note. And how getting himself arrested had seemed the only way to get to the police station.

Sergeant Smith interrupted him. "You mean, someone vandalized and burned your fence? And the fire was originally headed for *your* house?"

Uncle Philbert nodded seriously.

"Do you have any idea who might have set the fire?"

"Let me put it this way: it's gotta be a feller who doesn't have a whole lot goin' on upstairs." Uncle Philbert tapped his head with a meaningful look. "Someone who most likely didn't reckon on the wind spreading the fire, especially not toward *his* house."

"Any idea who that might be?"

"I suspect it's the same feller who made the anonymous phone call, once the fire turned around and started headin' his way."

The policeman pulled a file off his desk. "It says here you've had some trouble with a neighbor's dog killing your sheep. Would this be that same neighbor?"

"Might be," said Uncle Philbert.

"Do you want to bring charges against him?"

"No, sir, I don't. First off, I ain't got no proof. Second, I don't believe in settling stuff with lawyers. And third, if ever I was to meet him face-to-face, why, I'd have to thank him."

"*Thank* him?"

"Sure," said Uncle Philbert with a slow grin. "Why, burning's the best thing you can do to a field after you got the crop in. It's great for the soil. In the old days, all the farmers did it. These days it ain't permitted no more. So I reckon when I get home I'll send that feller a thank-you note." He got to his feet. "Well, Matilda, are you ready to go home?"

The sergeant's face brightened at this. "Yes," he said quickly. "We'd be happy to drop all charges. In fact, I bet Officer Jones would even give you a ride home. Maybe he'll even round up your horse for you."

"Yes," said Officer Jones. "I'd be very happy—"

"Oh no," said Aunt Matilda, sitting down and picking up her knitting. "This is the most interesting thing that's happened to me since I don't know when. I'm not leaving. I haven't started my tunnel. Or finished Sergeant Smith's mittens. It's just bad form to leave in the middle of something—"

But Uncle Philbert had entered the cell, grasped Aunt Mattie firmly by the elbow, and started leading her, still talking, out of the building, followed by Parker and Officer Jones.

"—and I haven't made my one phone call yet, because of course our phone isn't actually plugged in—our phone at home, I mean: the police officer's phone is working fine—and I couldn't think who else to call. Did you know, Bertie dear, that you really *do* have a right to one phone call? And I have a right to a lawyer and—"

"Matilda," said Uncle Philbert firmly. "Did you know you also have the right to remain silent?"

"Yes, fascinating, isn't it? I—"

"It's a right," said Uncle Philbert, "that you ought to exercise more often."

Lawnicide

"If you know who set the fire, why didn't you tell the police?"

Uncle Philbert selected a fat piece of wood, stood it on its end, and shouldered the sledgehammer. "Like I said, I don't hold with telling on folks, especially if you ain't got proof. Here, now, keep the wedge in the center of the log. Good."

Parker held the splitting wedge in place while Uncle Philbert tapped the top of it a few times with the sledgehammer, until it was set in the wood.

"Let go," Uncle Philbert commanded. "And stand back." Hoisting the heavy tool over his head, he took aim and brought the sledgehammer down with a hard metallic *thunk*, driving the wedge halfway into the wood. A few more blows, and the log flew into two pieces. Parker gathered them up. "You can start a new pile there behind the kitchen."

"Maybe you should go and talk to him," said Parker, after he'd deposited the logs. That's what you were supposed to do at school with a bully—tell him it hurts your feelings, boo hoo.

"Tried that. He's not the kind you can talk to."

Tell me about it, thought Parker. "Did you try using 'I messages'?"

"What's that?" Uncle Philbert lined up a new log, and Parker placed the wedge in the center of it.

"Instead of saying, 'You're a jerk for letting your dog kill my sheep,' or whatever, you're supposed to say, 'When you let your dog kill my sheep, I feel sad.'"

"And that works better?"

"That's the idea, yeah."

Uncle Philbert tapped the wedge into the wood. "Okay," he said. "Next time we meet that neighbor, I'm gonna say, 'When you let your jeezly dog kill my sheep'"—he brought the sledgehammer down with a *thud*—"'or set my field on fire, I feel madder than a boiled owl.'" *Thud.* "'I also feel like frog-marching you down to the county jail, tossing you into a small, unheated cell'"—*thud*—"'and puttin' the key somewhere where the sun don't shine.' How about that?"

"Yeah. That's good. But seriously, Uncle Philbert. He's trying to scare you off your land, force you to sell. What are you going to do about it?"

Uncle Philbert worked in silence for a moment, then stopped to wipe his brow. "The way I figger it, I been here fifty years. I'm gonna just plain outlast 'em," he said, and shouldered the sledgehammer again.

Parker said nothing. In his experience, if bullies weren't stopped, things usually went from bad to worse. But he could think of nothing to say to Uncle Philbert.

He turned back to his work and put the whole thing

out of his mind. The work was hard and repetitive and slow, but it had the advantage of stopping you from thinking too much. Over and over again, Parker bent to hold the wedge while Uncle Philbert tapped it into the log. Stood back and watched him drive the wedge. Gathered up the split wood. Carried it behind the house to stack. Back and forth he went. Back and then forth again.

Flies from the barn buzzed around his head in infuriating clouds and bit his exposed skin. The sun burned the back of his neck, and sweat stained his T-shirt. His thumbs were starting to blister, he had at least three splinters in his hands, and his mouth felt like a piece of dry toast.

Parker thought about the big bottle of SPF 45 sunscreen and the insect repellent his mother had packed for him. He thought about the remains of the six-pack of soda in his suitcase. At one point he thought about pointing out to Uncle Philbert that the whole activity was kind of pointless: Wood was wood, wasn't it? So why bother turning it into matchsticks before you burn it? He thought about telling him that maybe everyone should stop living like they were in an episode of *Little House on the Prairie* and join the twenty-first century. Buy some bundles of wood somewhere. The mall, for example. They must have wood for sale.

He thought about telling Uncle Philbert that his arms ached and he was hungry and thirsty and there were things he'd rather do than stack wood. Or worse, restack wood, which is what he had to do when the pile he was building suddenly slumped to the ground, just as it began to reach a respectable size. When he realized he would have to rebuild the whole pile from scratch, he thought of telling Uncle Philbert he couldn't go on another minute, that he was done for the day.

But instead, he let Uncle Philbert show him the trick of stacking the end pieces of each row crisscross, to make sturdy columns that would hold up the middle of the rows, keeping them from collapsing. And he said none of the things he was thinking. Maybe it was because the pathetic truth was that he didn't have anything better to do than to stack wood. Maybe it was because, after a little practice, the two of them had gotten into a kind of perfect, wordless rhythm, each one doing his job smoothly and efficiently so that the work flowed from one to the other, from the sledgehammer to the wedge to the rows of split logs. Maybe it was the sight of Uncle Philbert, his sleeves rolled up above his scrawny, whiplike arms, taking frequent rests to lean on the sledgehammer and mop his face with the red bandanna. Maybe it was a strange feeling of pleasure at the sound of the sledgehammer, the smell of freshly split wood, and the sight of the growing pile of neatly stacked firewood, the surprisingly tidy, surprisingly tall pile of neatly stacked firewood.

Whatever the reason, he said nothing. He pulled his cap over his eyes and tied the bandanna Uncle Philbert had given him around his neck to keep off the sun. He slid on the work gloves he'd been too proud to wear when he had started. And he kept on stacking.

He even, at one point while Uncle Philbert was taking a break, asked if he might have a go at using the sledgehammer. Uncle Philbert allowed as how he might, if he was very careful. He showed him the proper technique, and held the wedge for him until it was set in the wood. Parker's first few hammer blows were short and timid, and as often as not he missed the wedge and slammed the head of the hammer into the log, which sent shocks of pain vibrating up his wrists all the way to his shoulders. The first time this happened, he dropped the sledgehammer and yelped, shaking his numb hands.

Uncle Philbert only said, "Stings like a banshee, don't it?" and reached over and held out the sledgehammer to him. Parker, who'd been on the verge of calling it quits, was surprised to find himself reaching silently for the hammer. He wasn't going to let the old man think he was a quitter. He swung the hammer once more, and this time he made contact. A few more tries, and the log split neatly down the middle. The sight of the splintered wood gave him a ridiculous, secret thrill of pride. The second log took only two blows to split. Three logs later, by swinging the sledgehammer in a long arc behind his back and high over his head and by keeping his eyes glued to the metal wedge, he was able to shatter the wood with the first strike. Even Uncle Philbert hadn't been able to do that!

Finally the last of the wood was split. Uncle Philbert sat down on a log. Parker was surprised to see how winded his great-uncle was. This wood-splitting business was hard work, even for grown men.

"Time to go fishing?" asked Parker.

Uncle Philbert wiped the sweat off his forehead. "Time to mow the lawn," he said.

Parker couldn't believe his ears. He was half dead, and so was Uncle Philbert, he was sure. "But what about the mower?" he asked.

As far as Parker could tell, the lawn mower had long ago been "euthanized"—put permanently to sleep—along with a motley assortment of furniture and machines that Aunt Mattie and Uncle Philbert had taken from the house or barn and placed in the front yard. When he'd asked her about this earlier, Aunt Mattie had admitted to him that she found most furniture quite boring.

"Chairs. Tables. They ask very little of you," she explained, "and they give you very little back in return."

"What do you mean?" asked Parker.

"They don't throw you surprise birthday parties. They don't need help with algebra homework. They seldom offer to take out the garbage." As a result, she explained, she tended to leave unwanted furniture outdoors to die a peaceful death, rather than keep it inside where you might well stub your toe on it, where you had to dust it or think about it.

That would explain the hideous wooden bed now being used as a roost for the peacocks. And an overstuffed armchair that Aunt Mattie said had "refused to listen to reason," which was being slowly unstuffed by a variety of wildlife, both plant and animal, that had found refuge in its innards.

Then there were the machines. Most were victims of Uncle Philbert's strange mechanical "black thumb": a lawn mower with a broken starter handle that he had repeatedly destroyed and finally given up on. A vacuum cleaner that blew out instead of sucking in. A chain saw with a busted chain.

"That's a funny story," Uncle Philbert had said when Parker asked him about the chain saw, that first day on the farm. "A few years ago I had a tree come down that was too big for any of my saws." (Parker had seen those saws hanging on the wall of the barn—long, two-handled push-me-pull-you thingies with rows of huge, sharp teeth.) "So I went down street to Sears and Roe-buck—"

"I think it's just called Sears these days."

"—so I went to Sears and Roebuck and told the young feller there in the tool department that I needed a saw that could take care of a big old baister of a tree. He pulled out that saw you see right there. 'Looks kinda runty to me,' I say to him. 'I misdoubt it can han-dle a big tree.'

" 'No problemo,' he says to me, all cocksure. 'It'll turn anything into kindling in minutes, or your money back.'

"So I take that saw, and I saw away on that tree. But by the end of the day, I've only cut up three small branches. I go back and tell that feller, 'Seems to me you sold me a crate o' flapdoodle. Told me a stretcher.' "

Seeing Parker's puzzled look, Uncle Philbert trans-lated. "That was just my polite way of telling him he was being frugal with the truth. Hornswogglin' me. Oh, all right—*lyin'*. I tell him the saw don't work and I want my money back. He takes the chain saw and gives a yank on the handle. Straightaway that saw gives a big roar, and the chain starts spinnin' around.

" 'There,' he says. 'It works perfect.'

" 'Whoa, Nelly,' I say to him. 'What's that *noise?*' "

Parker looked blank.

" 'Whoa, Nelly,' I say to him. 'What's that *noise?*' " Uncle Philbert repeated patiently.

Parker still looked blank.

"It's a joke, son." Philbert sighed. "Never mind."

It was two days before Parker got the joke, and it came to him during lunch, in midswallow. His laughter quickly turned into choking and snorting. He put down his glass of blue lemonade. *"What's that noise?"* he gasped. "Now I get it."

"Two days to get a joke. The boy's quick," said Uncle Philbert to Aunt Mattie. Then he peered closely at Parker. "And look at that—he's gone and done the nose trick. I take back what I said about your school. They do teach you useful stuff."

Parker realized that he had, in fact, laughed so hard he'd managed to spray blue lemonade out his nose. "YOMANK, dude," he said, wiping his face.

"Yomank?"

"Don't they teach you anything in school these days?" asked Parker smugly, enjoying Uncle Philbert's puzzled look. "You Owe Me A New Keyboard. It's like the modern way to say 'nose trick.' Like when you're in the middle of drinking a soda and someone IMs you something that makes you LOL and you spew all over your keyboard."

100

"Keyboard? Are we talkin' pianos here?"

"IM?" asked Aunt Mattie. "LOL?"

Parker sighed. "Never mind," he said.

"Besides the mower," Parker continued as Uncle Philbert was catching his breath after splitting the wood, "I have a second question. Where's the lawn?"

Uncle Philbert walked with Parker to the front yard. In truth, there wasn't much lawn, just a little grass sprouting in one corner near some apple trees. Mostly it was wildflowers and moss.

"That's all there is," admitted Uncle Philbert. "Why would I want any more? Why would anyone?"

Parker puzzled a bit over this. Until he gave up and hired a lawn service, his father had devoted a huge amount of time and money to his lawn. Half his time was spent trying to get grass to *grow*: planting grass seed, watering it, fertilizing it, spreading lime dust, spraying poisonous chemicals, installing underground sprinkler systems. The other half was spent trying to get grass to *stop* growing: cutting it with a riding mower, trimming it with a weed whacker, pulling it out of gardens.

"Lawns—phooey! You know why lawns were first invented?" Uncle Philbert asked.

"No." He didn't really care, either, so long as he didn't have to mow them.

"A hundred years ago nobody had lawns." Apparently Parker was going to hear about lawns whether he wanted to or not. "They had crops planted on every inch of their land. Then one day some rich feller gets a notion to plant some of his land with useless stuff—grass—just to show his neighbors that he's *so* rich he don't *need* to plant his land in crops. A hundred years later, we all do it, like lemmings jumping off a cliff together. Me, I'm trying to kill my lawn."

Parker just nodded dumbly. If Aunt Mattie spent her time killing unwanted furniture, it seemed to make perfect sense that Uncle Philbert would devote himself to killing his own lawn. "So . . . where's the lawn mower?" he asked.

"Right here." Philbert disappeared into the farmhouse and reemerged a few minutes later leading Buster on a long rope. "Let me show you how to mow the lawn." He took a screw-shaped metal stake, attached Buster's rope to it, and screwed it into the ground. "Presto. All done!" he said, stepping back and taking in the sight. "Buster is old enough now to be outdoors and eat real grass. And she's the perfect lawn mower: self-propellin', never needs to have her blade sharpened. Never needs gas or oil. Never breaks down. Nonpollutin'. Fertilizes as she goes," he finished, removing Buster's diaper as he talked and looking very pleased with himself. "You just need to move the stake every few hours." He passed the rope to Parker. "It'll be the easiest lawn you never mowed."

But as it turned out, Uncle Philbert, who was right about so many things, couldn't have been more wrong about the lawn.

Fraidy Cat

Hisssss

The fishing that afternoon was sweet. In the last few days, Parker had been to the stream almost every day. Sometimes he went alone, and sometimes Uncle Philbert came with him and sat whittling a piece of wood and talking. Some days he swam in the cold water. Or he caught frogs and minnows with a fine-mesh net. One day Uncle Philbert dug a homemade turtle trap, constructed from an old orange crate, out of a corner of the barn and showed him how to catch the painted turtles that sunned themselves on rocks and fallen trees along the edges of the broad pool.

But mainly he worked on perfecting his casting technique. As the days went by, he progressed from catching his own clothing, to catching tree branches, to landing the fly in the water, and then to landing it more or less where he wanted it. It was a proud day when Uncle Philbert let him graduate from casting corks to casting real flies.

But he had gotten used to casting without catching anything. In fact, for him, the real point of fishing was simply getting the fly to soar through the air to the exact spot he'd picked out on the water, kind of like target practice. He'd almost forgotten about the part where the fish takes the fly.

"Bugs are thicker 'n spatters today," Uncle Philbert announced as Parker was attaching a particularly colorful fly—which he had created the night before—to his line. "So are the trout. It should be like eatin' pie to catch one."

Parker had made a perfect cast and was congratulating himself on avoiding the low-hanging branches, when there was a sudden swirl of water next to his line, a flash of a huge black head reaching for the fly, and his rod tip bent nearly double. Parker had caught things before that doubled the rod up—weeds or branches or rocks. But this, this was something else entirely. Parker felt the living weight of the fish causing the line to thrum with life—so different from the feel of a line snagged on a deadweight. It was like a thrilling electric current running straight from the mouth of the fish up to his fingertips. It was as if he had the fish there in his hands.

As Parker stood frozen, watching the line rip through the water, Uncle Philbert yelled at him to keep his tip up, to pull on the line so as to set the hook in the trout's mouth. With a start, Parker came to life, pulling back on the rod and putting some drag on the old-fashioned reel by palming it with his right hand the way he'd seen Uncle Philbert do. The fish was so strong that the line continued to hiss out, the turning reel burning a hot circle into the flesh of his hand.

The fish fought him harder now, zigging and zagging

as it tried to lose the hook. Uncle Philbert was coaching him from across the pool. "Let it run a bit; don't pull too hard, or it'll bust the line. You got to tire it out. Give it some line. Stay with it. Stay with it."

So Parker gave the fish its head, trying to keep a steady pressure on the line. At one point he had to jump off the bank into the stream as the wily trout tried to take cover behind a large rock. Stumbling through the water, Parker tripped over a stone and went down. But he never let go of the rod or let up on the line. He came to the surface sputtering but holding the rod aloft triumphantly.

Parker had no idea how long he battled the trout—it felt like forever, up and down the stream bank, cranking line in and letting it out again. At last there came a

moment when he felt, he literally *felt* the trout give up. With Uncle Philbert's coaching, he reeled the line slowly in until he brought the exhausted fish right up to the edge of the pool. Uncle Philbert was waiting there with the net, ready to scoop the catch out of the water. Parker could see it now, just below the surface, straining against the rod and line. He could see the huge black back, scarred with white, the flashing eye, and the thrashing tail. The sight was so spectacular that as Uncle Philbert reached for the fish with the net, Parker let the rod sag, for just an instant. And that was all it took. The fish spat out the hook, whipped the water with its tail, and vanished. All that remained was Parker's line dangling limply, floating on the still, empty surface.

Parker looked at Uncle Philbert forlornly. He felt like an idiot. It was a long time before he could speak.

"Was that the Old Baister?" he asked.

"You better believe it." Uncle Philbert shook his head and clapped him on the back. "I oughta have taught you what to do when you get a strike like that. But I never once reckoned you'd catch a trout so quick—and the Old Baister at that. Boy, you sure have the knack, you do. Not half bad, for a city boy."

They had trout for dinner that night—three good-sized trout, two caught by Uncle Philbert, and one by Parker. Yes, he'd finally landed a trout. And instead of tossing them back, Philbert had showed him how to clean the fish. Then they'd brought them home for Aunt Mattie to fry up. Parker didn't like fish as a rule, and tried to beg off eating any, but he finally took a bite and discovered that fresh trout tastes unlike any other fish he'd ever eaten. He devoured an entire fish himself.

After dinner, his mind still on the afternoon fishing expedition, Parker came out to finish "mowing" the lawn. It took him a moment to locate Buster. She was cowering under an apple tree, staring wild-eyed into the distance. Her rope had wrapped itself tightly around the trunk of the tree, and she was hopping frantically up and down in an effort to disentangle it. It would have been a comical sight if Buster hadn't been so clearly terrified.

"Take it easy, Buster," Parker said as he bent to pull up the stake. "Help is on the way."

That's when he heard the sound.

It was a sound that raised the hair on the back of his neck and his arms. He turned around slowly and saw what Buster had been staring at. At first, in the dim light, he thought it was a wolf. The animal's upper lip was curled to show a row of strong white teeth. A low, gurgling growl came from deep in its throat, and its yellow eyes were fixed on Buster. It was not a wolf—but it was easily a hundred pounds of well-fed, well-groomed German shepherd with a shiny leather collar around its neck. And it looked like it had just found its next meal. Buster turned her terrified gaze on Parker and bleated pathetically.

Every single muscle and nerve fiber in Parker's body froze. He sent a command down to his legs, telling them to move. Useless. In the same way his old computer used to freeze up sometimes, refusing to respond to commands no matter how hard he pounded on the keyboard, his legs refused to answer. Parker had every intention of going to Buster's rescue. He pictured himself charging at the dog, grabbing a stick or waving his arms wildly to scare it off, and then scooping up Buster and carrying her to safety. But his legs—and arms—stayed absolutely put. He did nothing. The dog took a slow step, and then another, toward the terrified lamb. Then it crouched as if to spring.

"Buster," breathed Parker.

At that moment one of the cats—it looked like clueless little Fraidy Cat—walked between the lamb and the dog. Spying the German shepherd, Fraidy Cat let out an unearthly hiss and fluffed himself up like a bottle brush till he looked almost as big as a normal cat. He and the German shepherd stared at each other for a long moment, and then Fraidy Cat bolted, racing for a maple tree in a corner of the yard. The spell was broken. The dog gave a tremendous bark and surged off in hot pursuit of the terrified cat.

Parker watched just long enough to be sure that Fraidy Cat had made it safely into the tree, with the hound snapping vainly at the lower branches. Then his legs came back to life. He untied Buster and carried her inside the farmhouse, dropping her into her pen. He threw the mess of books and cats off the sofa and collapsed onto it, burying his head under some pillows.

What he really, really wanted right now was his Game Boy. Or something, anything, that he could turn on, plug into, to drown out the things he was thinking that he didn't want to be thinking. If he could only kill a few Space Monkeys right now, then he was sure he would stop seeing Buster's terrified eyes, the way she looked at him as if he could somehow help her. And he would stop remembering that time at the bus stop, the time last spring with Simon when the school bullies had come after them, and instead of protecting his younger cousin, he'd hidden in the bushes. And the time before that when—

Minesweeper. He had Minesweeper on his cell phone. Where the heck was his cell phone? Not in his pocket. Must have fallen out. What else could go wrong? What the heck else could go wrong?

He started ripping the cushions off the sofa, one by one, looking for his cell phone. The noise must have attracted Aunt Mattie and Uncle Philbert. They appeared at the door to the sitting room, in their bathrobes. Uncle Philbert had a toothbrush in one hand.

"Now, dear, what's got you in such a tizzy?" asked Aunt Mattie, replacing one of the sofa cushions.

Parker said nothing for a while. At last he dropped down onto the sofa, rested his head against the back of it, and, staring at the ceiling, told them about the German shepherd.

"I just stood there like a frozen Popsicle. I didn't try to rescue Buster. I didn't run away. I couldn't even do *that*. And who saves my butt? Useless, runty Fraidy Cat, that's who. How funny is *that*?"

"Well," said Uncle Philbert after a moment, "I think you did everything just right."

Parker gave him an angry look. "What?"

"First off, did your hair all stand up?"

Parker could still remember the feel of each hair on his body and head standing straight up—just like in some clichéd horror story. "Yeah. So what?"

"There's a good reason you do that. It's to make yourself look bigger to the animal that's threatening you. Ever notice how a cat's hair all stands up when it's threatened? You just did the same thing. Very smart of you."

Parker snorted at this—at the thought of him looking scary with his buzz cut standing on end. "Good for me," he said sarcastically. "I've got smart hair."

"Did you run away or did you stay still?"

"I told you, I was petrified." *Literally. Turned to stone. Pathetic.*

"Smart choice."

Parker gave him a disbelieving stare. Was he mocking him?

"No, I mean it," said Uncle Philbert. "You see, a predator is attracted by movement. Why, if you'd moved so much as an eyelash, if you'd threatened him, that dog might have gone for you—like he did with Fraidy Cat. And that dog's a nasty piece of work. Belongs to our neighbors. Probably the same one that killed Buster's mother."

"Oh, great. So I'm good at playing possum. I'm really *excellent* at being the deer frozen in the headlights. That's *real* brave."

"Hey, I didn't say you were brave. I said you were smart. Smart comes in lots of different flavors—not just book smarts. And sometimes smart beats brave."

Parker had to grin a little at that. Then, while Uncle Philbert went to check on Fraidy Cat, Aunt Mattie took Parker into the kitchen and fed him a big slice of rhubarb-strawberry-peach-plum pie. They all played Scrabble for a while, Fraidy Cat climbing halfway up Philbert's chest and purring like a pastry. And no one challenged Parker when he claimed *scumbly* was a word and he used all seven letters and won.

Or Else

"Not half bad, for a city boy."

It was strange how happy that backhanded compliment about fishing had made Parker feel. He was determined to actually catch the Old Baister the next time. But he would need to get up really early—when the fishing was best—to be at the stream first thing.

Parker had, by necessity, fallen into a rhythm of going to bed earlier and getting up earlier than he was used to in his "old" life. If he wanted to eat breakfast, and dinner, he had no choice but to do so. With supper served at five, staying up till midnight meant he was famished by the time he went to bed. And sleeping through breakfast meant he missed out on the doughnuts or chili or whatever Aunt Mattie had put on the table at the unthinkable hour of six o'clock.

But this morning he planned to get up even before breakfast. He could use the alarm clock feature on his cell phone (which had eventually turned up, under the sofa), but Uncle Philbert had told him his own never-fail system for waking up early without an alarm. You simply decide what time you want to wake up, and then before you go to sleep you bang your head that many times on the pillow. Parker was curious to try it, so he banged his head on the pillow five times, and when he woke next morning and checked his cell phone, it was exactly five o'clock. Parker, for the first time ever, was awake before anyone else.

He grabbed the pole, net, and tackle box and headed out through the pasture. A gentle drizzle sifted from the gray sky as he crossed the fields, in and out of gates. The walk, which had once seemed so long, was now familiar, and the time passed easily.

He was going over the motions of casting—one-two-three-four, the rod moving from ten o'clock to two o'clock as if it were an hour hand—when he heard an unexpected noise: shouts of laughter and loud popping sounds. He came out of his daydream and noticed two mud-spattered green ATVs parked in the path to the trout pool. They had clearly come down the ridge, across the stream, and over the hay field, tearing up the ground and leaving muddy gouges.

Parker scrambled to the edge of the pool. There, on the far side, were the two boys he'd seen here at the start of his vacation. This time there was also a girl with them, and a dog—the same German shepherd that had terrified Buster—tied to a tree next to the ATVs. The boys were poised on the big boulder, and they each had a BB gun. They were taking turns aiming at something in the water near the boulder. The girl sat on the shore, watching the two of them.

"You guys," she was saying, "this is really stupid. Let's go home."

113

"There he is!" shouted the younger boy, pointing at something under a rock. The bigger boy pumped his air gun excitedly, aimed, and fired. The pellet made a spurting sound as it plowed into the shallow water.

"Missed him," he said. "Wait! There he goes! Jeezum, he's freakin' huge!"

Parker stood by the opposite edge of the trout pool, frozen and horrified. The intruders hadn't seen him yet. The boy rolled another pellet into the breech of his air gun and pumped it five or six times. A kind of fury overtook Parker as he realized exactly what they were doing. Without thinking, he dropped the tackle, pulled out a length of line from his fly rod, flicked the tip of the rod back and forth in the air a few times, and launched a cast, just as the boy drew a bead on the water for a second time. He had done it all automatically, without conscious thought—making an allowance for the direction and strength of the wind, calculating the distance to the shore—and the cast was a perfect one. Before the boy could pull the trigger, he suddenly spun sideways, as if someone had shoved him, and fell into the water with a huge splash.

"What the heck!" he sputtered, emerging from the water without his gun and looking around accusingly. The younger boy and the girl were laughing uproariously. "You jerk, Connor. You pushed me in. You think that's funny, do you?" His voice cracked with anger, and he gave Connor a shove in the chest, knocking him to the ground. "I'll show you what's funny, you little—"

But the girl put a hand out to stop him. "What's this?" she asked, lifting up a piece of fishing line trailing behind the older boy. She gave a little tug. One end of the line was attached to a fishhook, neatly sunk into the side of the older boy's pants. She pulled on the other end, only to discover it was attached to nothing, Parker had quickly cut the line the moment he had "landed" his human trout. All three of them stared dumbly at the fish line, and then they turned and spotted Parker.

"It's that kid from the farm," said the older boy. He glared at Parker. "You creep!" Then he said to Connor, "Let's get him."

He started picking his way around the pool toward Parker. Connor gave him a sullen look but got slowly to his feet and followed. Parker felt all the bravado and anger drain from him like bathwater from a cold tub. He'd been in this situation a hundred times before—outnumbered by bigger kids—and he knew darn well what was going to happen next.

He backed up a few steps and stumbled over a rock, falling hard to the ground beside his fly rod. Seeing him fall, the older boy surged forward. Parker grabbed hold of the fly rod—he couldn't leave Uncle Philbert's precious rod behind—and stood up quickly, gripping the fishing pole in both hands. He saw both boys hesitate for a moment.

Seeing them falter gave Parker a measure of courage. He stopped backing up and tried to assess his situation. Yes, he was outnumbered, but the girl didn't look interested in fighting and neither, for that matter, did the younger boy. Connor, in fact, was still eyeing the older boy resentfully and lagging behind him.

Parker met the older boy's gaze and slowly pulled himself to his full height, brandishing the rod like a club, trying to make himself look as big as possible and praying no one could actually see his heart thudding against his chest under his T-shirt.

The older boy had stopped a dozen yards away. He jerked his head at Connor, but the younger boy ignored him, staying where he was. *It can't be,* thought Parker, *can it?* He took two small, experimental steps forward. The other boy took two small steps backward. Whoa! Maybe the boy *was* scared of him!

"This is private property," said Parker, with a confidence he was nowhere near feeling. "Go get your gun. And don't come back here."

Now's the part where they always snicker, *Or else what, Porker? Your grandma will beat us up? Porkie pie. Lard bucket.*

The boy scowled at him. "You better hope the gun isn't wrecked," he said at last. "Or else."

"Or else what?" Parker retorted, his voice more steady now. "Your little sister will hurt me?"

"Or else . . . you'll be sorry."

Parker was sure he saw both Connor and the girl start to giggle at this feeble response. The girl gave him what looked like a sympathetic smile, and he found himself smiling shyly in return. Then an even more amazing thing happened. The older boy turned to leave. He was not going to pound Parker into the ground. He was not going to make him into mince pie. He was leaving, running away, all of his taunts left unsaid. His attempt to stalk off angrily, with an intimidating glare, was badly undercut when he suddenly fell to the ground. Connor, it turned out, had been standing on the fish line, still trailing from the other boy's pants. The girl laughed out loud at this.

"You moron!" snarled the older boy to Connor. He gripped the fish line and tried to yank the hook out but succeeded only in tearing a huge hole in his pants. The girl covered her mouth to hide her giggles.

"Purple boxers," said Parker. "Nice."

The boy turned a furious shade of crimson. Cursing, he retrieved his gun and untied his dog, all while trying to hold his pants together with one hand. When he was a safe distance away, he turned to sneer at Parker.

"You'll be sorry. Just wait. My dad says you'll *all* be sorry. Especially your whacko great-uncle."

"Oh yeah?" said Parker. But the boy's words had sent an unexpected chill down his spine, and his attempt at bravado sounded hollow, even to his own ears.

Parker 911

Parker didn't mention the incident at the stream, or the thinly veiled threat, to his great-aunt or great-uncle. This time it wasn't because he was ashamed of his behavior. It was because the whole subject of the turnpike deal seemed to have become taboo. When each day's post brought some letter or other with Numitz Bilkum & Smattering's return address, Uncle Philbert simply fed it, unopened, into the cookstove. If it hadn't been for the letters, and the brief conversation they'd had while splitting wood, Parker might have thought he'd dreamed up Mr. Numitz's visit.

The only proof he had that Mr. Numitz had actually been there, in their kitchen, was the way Uncle Philbert and Aunt Mattie made fun of Mr. Numitz's city ways. It became a little game for them. Instead of drinking water, they "personally rehydrated" themselves. And everything became a "system." The dishwasher became the "dish-cleansing system," the cookstove was the "heating-and-food-preparation system," and so on.

That might be okay for them—making games out of

it—but it was driving Parker crazy. Not talking about something, he found, didn't make it go away. Like not dealing with bullies, it just made it worse. He was still trying to think of a way to tell Uncle Philbert about the incident at the trout pool several days later as the two of them were tinkering with the engine of a skinny old tractor (the same skinny tractor from the "Just Married" photo, Parker realized). The dust and grit of morning chores clung to their damp skin as mosquitoes tried to suck the last of their blood.

"Now we just attach this wire here," said Uncle Philbert, putting down the Stilson wrench, "and she'll be purring like a pastry. Hand me that screwdriver."

"I think you've got it backward," Parker said, examining the wiring.

"Are you trying to teach your grandmother how to suck eggs?"

"What?"

"It's a figger of speech. It means that someone who doesn't know the odds between a *brake* and a *clutch* shouldn't try to tell an *expert mechanic* how to fix an engine." He folded the engine cover shut and gave it a confident tap with the wrench.

"I may not know much about brake pedals," said Parker stoutly, "but I do know batteries, and believe me, you've got the wires—"

Too late. Uncle Philbert had reached up and pushed the tractor's starter. There was a muffled explosion, then wisps of smoke emerged from under the hood. Uncle Philbert pursed his mouth thoughtfully and tapped his fingers against the tractor.

120

"I wouldn't mention this to your aunt Mattie," he said at last.

Parker struggled not to laugh. He could practically hear Aunt Mattie calling Uncle Philbert a "stubborn old fool." He smiled and made the motion of zipping his lips shut. But as they began picking up their tools, he blurted out, "Speaking of stubborn, Uncle Philbert, Mr. Numitz was going to make you a millionaire. Why did you turn him down?"

Uncle Philbert turned and glared at Parker until Parker felt himself blushing. What? What had he said?

"Young whiffet," said Uncle Philbert after a moment, "what exactly could a million dollars buy me that I don't already have?"

Parker could think of a few things. "A new dishwasher. A boat. A condo in Florida. A new car." He wanted to add, but didn't, the new Xbox 360 video game "system."

Uncle Philbert shook his head. "Oh, you sound just like Mr. Dinglefuzzie with his crate of flapdoodle. And what would I do with all those things? Everything I need is right here in this valley. Now, let's go ketch us some trout. I'm dead certain the Old Baister is hungerin' for one of my hand-tied caddis flies this mornin'. A million dollars ain't goin' to make him bite my flies any faster."

As they passed through one of the crooked gates, Uncle Philbert had to sit a moment and catch his breath. It was only a few weeks ago, Parker noted with some surprise, that it was Parker who had had to sit here and catch *his* breath. This morning the four-mile hike hadn't left him the least bit winded. At last, Uncle Philbert hauled himself to his feet and they set off again. Although it was still early morning, it was already hot and muggy and both of them took their time.

As they approached the trout stream, Parker began to feel uneasy. Something was different. Something was wrong. He noticed a fresh set of ATV tracks, and his heart began to beat harder. Was that what was wrong? Were the kids from the neighbor's house lying in wait for them, up at the pool, with the BB gun? He became aware, suddenly, of what seemed off: there were no birds. No birds calling from the tops of trees. No swallows swooping over the pool to catch the flies and bugs that hovered above the surface. No birds hopping in the bushes that lined one side of the pool. And there were no fish jumping. Everything was deathly still.

He recalled the boys' warning that Uncle Philbert would be sorry one day, and for the hundredth time he debated whether to say something to his great-uncle. No. Uncle Philbert didn't want to talk about it, and it was stupid to worry about a couple of kids. He said nothing as he sat down on a rock and began the process of choosing a fly for his line. But the hairs on his arms were standing up as he did it.

"What do you think—the mayfly or the flying ant?" he asked as he pulled two flies out of the brim of his Red Sox cap. Uncle Philbert was standing by the side of the pool with his back to Parker, as he always did before they began fishing, checking out what kinds of flies were hatching. That was the real skill of fly fishing, Uncle Philbert always claimed, knowing which fly the fish were looking for that very minute. Yesterday the trout might have been tripping over each other, shoving and jostling like shoppers at a bargain-basement sale, to get at your caddis fly. But put that same caddis fly on your line the next morning, when all that was hatching out of the stream were spruce bud flies, and those trout would turn up their noses as if you'd offered them a rancid bit of rat poison.

"Or maybe we should tempt them with Parker's Patented Flapdoodle?" This was a fly that Parker had invented, using bits of peacock feather, tied to a hook with hair from Sugar's tail. He'd come up with the name because, as he explained to Uncle Philbert, getting a trout to bite a fake fly was basically the same thing as trying to sell it a crate of flapdoodle. "What do you think? . . . Uncle Philbert?"

He glanced up at his great-uncle, and something about the way he was standing, the slump of his shoulders, made Parker jump to his feet in alarm.

"What's wrong?" Still Uncle Philbert said nothing, and Parker scrambled over to his side, saw where he was looking, and felt his stomach do a little flip of shock.

The surface of the pool was dotted with dozens of pale slivers of different sizes. The water they floated in, usually clear enough to see straight to the bottom, was filthy with silt. Parker bent down and picked up one of

123

the white slivers. It was a young trout, dead and limp. The white slivers were all trout, dozens of them, floating belly-up.

He looked at his great-uncle. Uncle Philbert was just standing there, staring. His face had gone pale under his tan, and his mustache was quivering.

"What happened?" asked Parker, his voice a hoarse whisper.

"Some fool," said Uncle Philbert at last, and it seemed to Parker he was having trouble catching his breath, "some low-down, piss-poor, yellow-bellied son of a sea cook has been and dynamited the pool."

"What? Why?"

"Why? To kill all the fish, of course. It's less bother than using a rod. Dynamite: the poor fisherman's friend."

"But they didn't even take the fish," objected Parker, looking at the lifeless trout speckling the surface.

"That's the puzzlin' part. Perhaps they did it for the entertainment value. More fun than shootin' fish in a barrel." He shook his head.

"Or as a threat," said Parker, without thinking.

Uncle Philbert fixed him with a stern, questioning look, and Parker saw that there was no way out of telling him.

"I saw the kids from the neighbor's house here, a couple of days ago. They were trying to shoot the Old Baister. And they told me that you were going to be sorry. I think they were talking about if you didn't sign the turnpike deal."

When he finished, he regretted having spoken, noting with alarm that Uncle Philbert's face had grown even paler and he was breathing hard.

"Uncle Philbert, you better sit down," said Parker, and he grabbed his great-uncle's sleeve. "Come on, come and sit down."

"I'll do that," said Uncle Philbert. "Just for a minute." He followed Parker over to a shady spot, lowered himself heavily to the ground, lay back against a rock with a sigh, and closed his eyes.

Parker watched him for a while, then asked the question that was uppermost in his mind. "Do you . . . do you think the Old Baister got away okay?" He must have, somehow, found a safe spot. He was, after all, nearly immortal.

Uncle Philbert shook his head. "I'm afraid not, son. They're all dead."

"But you don't know for sure—"

"I do," he said without opening his eyes. "I spotted him straightaway. Hard to miss, he's so big. He's right up by the big boulder."

Parker looked around for the long-handled net and picked his way over to the boulder. And there he was: unmistakable, his pale spotted belly at least twice the size of any of the others. Parker clambered onto the rock and scooped him into the net. The Old Baister was so heavy that even in death he nearly tipped Parker into the pool as he struggled to lift the net free of the filthy water.

He brought the Old Baister back and put him silently on the ground before Uncle Philbert. He was a gorgeous fish—battle-scarred skin speckled orange and yellow below, shading to a dark shiny black on top—and surprisingly soft to handle.

"Will we eat him, Uncle Philbert?" asked Parker after a while.

"Eat the Old Baister? Nossir. You know the rule."

Parker nodded, relieved. *You can't eat anything with a name.* "We'll take him home and give him a proper burial, then." He picked up the old trout and slid him into the picnic basket. The fish was so large that his tail and part of his body stuck out. For some reason this bothered Parker, and it also bothered him that bits of grass and dirt had stuck to the great fish's body. He tried to brush them off and to arrange the trout so that he fit more comfortably into the basket.

"Let's go, Uncle Philbert," said Parker, anxiously. Suddenly he didn't want to be here, with all the dead fish. He wanted to be home with Aunt Mattie, eating one of her strange pies, drinking her famous blue lemonade and telling jokes around the kitchen table. "Come on." He tugged on his sleeve. But Uncle Philbert just sat there, with his eyes closed.

"Come on, Uncle Philbert," he said, more urgently. This was no time to be taking a nap. "Let's go home." But Uncle Philbert didn't move, even when Parker squeezed his hand and shook him, he didn't move, and Parker stood up, scared. He backed away a few steps, his breath coming in ragged little hiccups and his mind racing.

"Don't be scared." Saying it out loud, whispering it—"Don't be scared"—as if that might help.

Why not? The answering voice in his head, the voice

that's always ready with a put-down. *Being scared is what I'm good at.*

No. Be brave.

I can't. I'm no good at brave. I'm a coward.

Run away, then. At least you can do that. Go for help. Run!

I can't even run. It's four miles to the farmhouse, at least—if I could run that far. And I can't.

If he were a good, brave Boy Scout—if he hadn't dropped out of Boy Scouts because of the usual reasons—he would know what to do now. Boy Scouts know how to send for help—how to send smoke signals or use mirrors or semaphores or whatever. But he isn't a Boy Scout. And he doesn't feel brave.

Sometimes, says a new voice in his head—his great-uncle's voice—*sometimes smart beats brave.* Okay, then. He can be smart. *Smart comes in lots of different flavors.* Wait a minute. Smoke signals? Mirrors? He doesn't need smoke signals: he has a freakin' cell phone! He can call 911!

He pulls it out of his pocket. It takes forever to power on. And then . . . *no service.* He hates that No Service icon with a deep hideous passion and has to fight the urge to throw the hateful cell phone into the trout stream. A temper tantrum is not going to help Uncle Philbert. *Think, you fool. Think.*

Be smart.

Sometimes you can get a better signal if you get to higher ground.

He looks at the ridge behind the pool and then he just starts running. Thank God for the ATV tracks.

They make a path he can climb instead of having to bushwhack through the woods. It is straight-up running, straight up the side of the ridge. It takes forever, and he is intensely aware that there is no inhaler in his pocket. He has a picture in his head of his inhaler sitting at the bottom of the trout pool. If his throat starts to close up, there will be no way to stop it. But he can't think about that right now. Panicking will just make it worse. He hasn't *really* needed the inhaler for ages. Maybe he no longer needs it at all. He holds on to that thought and keeps going. Panting, stumbling, falling, scraping his knees, but getting up each time and plunging back up the hill. He is amazed at how fast he is able to go, amazed that his legs hold out, and for a fleeting moment he wishes his old gym teacher could see him, the same gym teacher who mocked him when he couldn't do the wind sprints, the gym teacher who inspired his middle school classmates to new heights of ridicule by dubbing him "Porker" and "Pokey."

At the top, at last. Holding the cell phone over his head. One signal bar. One! Is that enough? He dials 911. It is ringing! Faintly, wobbly—but ringing.

"Nine one one," says a distant, scratchy female voice. "What is your emergency?"

"My great-uncle's sick," says Parker, gasping for breath. But it's not asthma—he's just plain winded from running like a maniac. He's pretty sure it's not asthma. "I think he's having . . . a heart attack or something."

"A what?"

"A heart attack."

"What?"

"*A heart attack!*"

"Hello? I can't hear you. Are you there?" The signal dies. And even though Parker stands there screaming into the phone, it does no good. She is gone.

Craptastic! He needs more signal. He has to get higher up. Parker looks around desperately. Can he climb a tree? Doubtful. Then he sees it.

The water tower.

He is at the foot of the tower in a minute, grasping the ladder that runs up one of the legs to the base of the tank. He is pulling himself up at top speed, using his arms to spell his tired legs, which have begun to tremble with fatigue.

In a minute or so he is at the narrow platform that makes a skirt around the base of the water tank. He holds out the phone. Still only one bar. Parker looks straight up. A second ladder continues up the side of the tank itself to the very top—only this ladder is really narrow, half the size of the first ladder. No matter. There has to be a stronger signal up there. He grabs the ladder and squeezes himself up it, one step at a time. Up and up. Then he's at the final rung and pulling himself belly-down onto the top of the water tower. He kicks away from the edge and keeps going, hands and knees, up the gentle angle of the sloping roof until he is holding the lightning rod that rises from the center, the tip top of the roof. He stands up, clutching the rod and grabbing into his pocket for the phone. Finally finds it. Flicks it open.

Two bars.

In moments he has the 911 lady again—loud and clear this time. Parker is panting for breath, can barely talk.

She is—to use one of Uncle Philbert's favorite expressions—calm as a clock.

"Take a deep breath," she says, "and tell me what your address is."

"I . . . don't know the address," Parker says, and looks around in a panic.

"What's your phone number? We can use it to look up the address," says the nice calm lady.

"I don't know the phone number. I'm on a cell phone."

"Okay, then." The nice calm lady is unflappable. "What's your great-uncle's name? We'll look up his address."

But Parker suddenly realizes all this discussion is useless. "I'm not at the house right now. I'm . . . I'm standing on a water tower." His heart sinks. Even if they can find him, what good will an ambulance be in the middle of the woods? Suddenly he has an idea. He knows about this from TV. "Can you send a helicopter? Like on *Chopper 911*?"

"You're standing . . . *on a water tower*??" says the lady, who sounds just a little bit less like a nice calm clock. She takes a moment to digest this information. "Can you describe where you are?"

For the first time, Parker looks around him, at the landscape below. Behind him stretch miles of woods and Uncle Philbert's green pastures, the stream, the distant farmhouse with its long dirt driveway, and, be-

131

yond that, the turnpike, its six lanes barely visible as it cuts through more fields and forests.

But in front of him, on the other side of the ridge, lies . . . *civilization*. Acres of tightly packed houses sprouting in rows like corn. Acres of pavement filled with boxy stores, shopping centers, and gas stations. Last of all, the mall: a maze of flat windowless buildings encircled by a vast parking lot full of gleaming metal and chrome. All of it lapping at the foot of the ridge like a shiny, glittering sea.

And the only thing standing between the turnpike behind him and the shopping mall in front of him is his great-uncle's farm. The farm—and the neighbor's house sitting high on the ridge. No wonder they want to build the turnpike exit ramp through here.

Parker is able to describe his exact location to the 911 lady: a blue water tower on the green splotch located between the turnpike and the shopping mall. And then, nicely, calmly, she says she'll try to send a helicopter.

Parker is standing, arm still hooked around the lightning rod, before he realizes his mistake. *Idiot. Moron.* He has told the 911 helicopter to come to *him*, to this ridge, instead of to Uncle Philbert, to the trout pool. That will waste all kinds of time, and he's sure that every single second counts.

He reaches for his lifeline, his cell phone, to call the 911 lady back again. Too urgently. The phone squirts from his sweaty fingers. It skitters slowly down the roof, right to the edge, where it seems to hesitate be-

132

fore taking the plunge. There are a few moments of silence before Parker's ears detect the sound of cell phone meeting hard granite, the unmistakable sound of expensive plastic being reduced to inexpensive junk.

Three things occur to Parker at that moment: (1) The cell phone is toast. (2) He has no choice now but to climb down off the tower as fast as possible and try to intercept the helicopter himself. And (3) where he's standing, right now, right here, is *a million freakin' feet off the ground.*

The adrenaline rush that propelled him up the tower with the force of a tidal wave has suddenly ebbed, and Parker sees the ground stretched out below him, way *way* below him, as if for the first time. He gets that feeling in his gut, that Empire State Building feeling. Only this time there is nothing—no high fence, no inch-thick windowpanes—between him and falling off the edge of the world.

His legs go liquid, he sits down with a thud, and then he turns over onto his stomach, one arm still clamped around the rod. He presses his face, his whole body into that roof, as if by doing so he might glue himself there.

A normal person would walk to the edge of the roof, firmly and fearlessly grasp the upright arms of the ladder that stick up above the roofline, turn confidently around, step backward off the roof into nothingness, and lower himself down the ladder.

Parker, on the other hand, knows there is no way he can walk down that roof, or go down that ladder. Not if his life depended on it.

He starts going to Plan B. Plan B involves a complicated rescue, of him, Parker, because Uncle Philbert does not seem that urgent right now. It's the kind of rescue that *Chopper 911* does so well, with a helicopter dangling ropes down to the water tower and lifting him, Parker, to safety. He has just gotten to the part where he is imagining hooking himself into the safety harness when he sees, beside his right hand, some graffiti scratched deep into the wooden base of the pole. It is a large heart with "Bertie Loves Mattie" and a date from the previous century. It has been painted over several times, but the writing is still clear.

Up until this moment Parker has been trying desperately hard not to think about Uncle Philbert and what is wrong with him. Or about Aunt Mattie and whether she will worry when they don't come home.

He starts to cry, and in a funny way that helps. As he cries, he starts backing toward the ladder. He doesn't stand or think about standing or even really think about what he's doing. He just does it. If he's thinking about anything, he's thinking about Uncle Philbert saying *Scared the bejeezus out of me.*

He slithers backward on his belly, every now and then risking a glance over his shoulder. His right foot strikes one of the ladder arms, his left foot finds the other one, and he keeps going. He keeps inching backward, both his legs now sticking through the ladder uprights, until his feet and shins are hanging out in the nothingness. The weight of his legs is trying to drag him off the roof, but he's holding on to that roof with his stomach and his arms and his fingernails and the skin of his face, while his legs and feet flail around trying to find that tiny narrow ladder. The only thing that can keep him from sliding off the tower right now is the two arms of the ladder that stick up above the roofline. But he can't reach them yet with his hands. He just knows that as he starts to slide, he will make a grab for them when he goes past.

Then suddenly his feet are down. Touching the first rung. His hands have found the ladder struts. He is there. He has done it. He keeps his eyes turned up and lets his feet find their own way down the long ladder. His legs are shaking, but his feet are working, almost on their own. They find the next rung and the next and the next.

When the helicopter finds him, he is dancing around the meadow like a madman, waving his Red Sox cap, pointing to Uncle Philbert, and doing jumping jacks to make sure they see him. His breath comes in ragged jerks, and he's still crying as the LifeFlight helicopter circles in and lands in the field below.

Pshaw

"It says here that visiting hours are from three to six."

Aunt Mattie paused in her packing as Parker read from the hospital pamphlet. " 'No visiting except during visiting hours. No cell phones. No two-way radios. No—' "

"Oh, pshaw," said his great-aunt. Parker had never actually heard somebody say *pshaw* before, and she pronounced it just the way it was spelled. "I'm well aware of the rules. I always leave the cell phone and the two-way radio at home." She handed the pamphlet back to Parker and returned to her packing. "But I can't see anywhere that says I can't bring a parrot. Can you?"

Parker looked at her, looked at the pamphlet, and grinned. "No," he said. "Not a word about parrots."

Rude . . .

Now that he knew there was a mall nearby, Parker made Aunt Mattie stop there on the way to the hospital, to let him buy something he told her he urgently needed; but they still arrived long before official visiting hours.

His great-aunt paused at the nurses' station, placing her packages on the floor.

"Good morning, Mrs. Bellwether," Aunt Mattie said to a woman sitting at the desk wearing a nurse's cap. "And how does your corporosity seem to gashiate today?"

"Extremely well, Mrs. Maxwell!" replied Mrs. Bellwether. She gave Aunt Mattie a big smile and leaned over the counter to peer at all the things Aunt Mattie was carrying. "What have you brought us today?"

"First of all, I've brought this fine young man for his first visit. He is my great-nephew. I know it's a little early, but he is anxious to see his great-uncle."

Parker nodded self-consciously at the nurse and two or three others who had crowded around his great-aunt.

"And I was hoping you would try out these butter-scotch chocolate chip cookies and let me know if you think they have quite enough butterscotch in them." She produced a tin of still-warm cookies, and the nurses took them gratefully.

"As for the rest of this . . ." She gestured to the various containers.

Mrs. Bellwether covered her ears and said, "I think I'm better off not knowing." She gave Aunt Mattie a wink.

"How is Uncle Philbert?" asked Parker, needing to know, needing to hear it from someone besides Aunt Mattie.

Mrs. Bellwether rolled her eyes. "His corporosity is gashiating quite nicely today."

Aunt Mattie looked at Parker. "I told you, your great-uncle is tough as a pitch knot." She looked at the head nurse. "And is he behaving himself?"

Mrs. Bellwether just laughed. "He's a sweetheart," she said.

Aunt Mattie smiled. "I won't tell him you said that. It will ruin his reputation. He thinks he's the rudest man in the world."

Mrs. Bellwether snorted. "If he thinks that," she said, watching a doctor approaching from the other end of the corridor, "all I can say is, he's got a lot of competition." She winked again at Aunt Mattie. Then to Parker she said, "Here comes Dr. Haley himself. You can ask him about your uncle."

Dr. Haley, a tall man with a mane of silver hair, marched up to the nurses' station, followed by a flock

138

of medical students and young doctors hastening to keep up.

"All right," he said, looking at a clipboard and not acknowledging Aunt Mattie or the nurses. "Next up: Quadruple Bypass in Room 203, and then"—he jerked his head toward Uncle Philbert's room—"Pacemaker in Room 204."

"Dr. Haley—" began Aunt Mattie, once he had finished.

"You are who?" he asked.

"I'm Mrs. . . . Pacemaker," she answered evenly. "I was wondering if you could tell me whether—"

As she was talking, Dr. Haley's pager went off. He unclipped it from his waistband, glared at it, reached over the counter, and grabbed the desk phone out of the hand of a nurse who was making a call. He dialed a number, turning his back on Aunt Mattie. When he finished, Aunt Mattie opened her mouth to speak again, but his pager went off once more and he held up an index finger before she could get a word out.

"Busy just now," snapped Dr. Haley. "Catch me later." Then he walked away. Parker and Aunt Mattie looked at each other.

"See what I mean?" said Mrs. Bellwether. "Rudest man on earth."

"This should be interesting," said Aunt Mattie.

Ruder . . .

When Parker walked into the room, Uncle Philbert was watching TV, staring intently at a set suspended from the ceiling. It was a morning talk show, with a particularly excitable bevy of guests shouting at each other.

"Will ya look at that?" he asked in a tone of disbelief, hardly glancing at Parker and Aunt Mattie. "They found some guys who will go on TV in front of millions of people and admit that they . . . they . . . Well, I'm too embarrassed even to say it out loud." He watched, open-mouthed, as the smiling talk-show host thanked his guests and then turned to the camera and said, "Have you ever eaten roadkill? Would you like to be on national TV? Call our toll-free number and you, too, could be a guest on the next—"

Uncle Philbert clicked the television off in disgust.

Parker looked from the TV to his great-uncle. Aunt Mattie had tried to convince him over the last few days that Uncle Philbert was fine. That he hadn't had a heart attack—that he'd only passed out at the trout stream because his heart was beating too slowly. That it was all fixed now. But Parker had needed to see for himself.

At the moment he didn't know which was more un-settling: the sight of his great-uncle with tubes and wires coming out of him like some sort of robo-uncle, or the sight of Uncle Philbert watching television. They kind of canceled each other out, he decided, sighing with relief. An Uncle Philbert who was watching TV had to be an Uncle Philbert who was going to be okay, wires and tubes or no wires and tubes.

"We brought you some company, and something to eat, like you asked, Uncle Philbert," Parker ventured.

He stashed the bigger objects beside Uncle Philbert's bed while Aunt Mattie hung a No Visitors sign on the door. Then she began unpacking the suitcase-like ob-ject that passed as her purse. It contained a bowl of Uncle Philbert's famous Twenty-Four-Alarm Chili and Beans, two slices of Right-Side-Up Cake (Aunt Mattie's upside-down version of Upside-Down Cake), some blue lemonade, and chocolate raspberry cookies.

"Breakfast!" said Uncle Philbert, smacking his lips eagerly and arranging the items on the little tray table that slid over his bed. "Praise the Lord. Because I mean to tell you, the food here all seems to come from the *Green Slime Cookbook*: lime Jell-O, pea soup, broc-coli puree. I druther eat maggot pie and sour owl urine. And they wouldn't let me order out for pizza. Imagine that." He'd just finished the chili when the door opened, and in swept Dr. Haley, like a comet, trailing his dust cloud of smaller, less important celes-tial objects—the students and junior doctors. He strode over to Uncle Philbert's bed and swept the food tray off to the side.

"I'm Dr. Haley," he announced, "your heart surgeon. Now then—"

"Dang," said Uncle Philbert, his fork poised above the spot where his Right-Side-Up Cake had so recently been. "Who ordered a heart doctor? I didn't. I ordered some pizza. You sure you're not the pizza guy?"

"No, I'm Dr. Haley—"

"And I'm tickled to meet you," continued Uncle Philbert. "Tickled as a cat with two tails. But I was just about to get down to some serious eatin'. Could you maybe come back later? Unless, of course, you brought pizza?" He looked hopefully at the medical students crowding around his bed, who were trying hard to smother grins.

Parker was sure, after glancing at Dr. Haley, that this was not the usual way the great man was greeted. The doctor ignored Uncle Philbert and turned to the students.

"You." He singled out a young woman on the other side of the bed whose smile was instantly replaced with a terrified expression. The young man next to her had a Teacher!-Teacher!-Call-on-me! look on his face and was clearly sorry to have been passed over. Parker disliked him instantly. "What are the symptoms of bradycardia?"

"Shortness of breath. Fatigue. Dizziness and fainting," said the young woman, looking like she herself might faint.

"Caused by?"

"Slow or irregular heartbeat."

"Treatment?" He pointed to the Teacher!-Teacher! guy.

"Insert a pacemaker to control the speed of the heartbeat," came the prompt answer.

Dr. Haley grunted. He seemed disappointed that he hadn't managed to catch anyone in an error.

Like someone following a Ping-Pong match, Uncle Philbert had been looking from Dr. Haley to the medical students as they talked back and forth over his head. "Hello? Remember me? I'm getting dizzy," he said. "And hungry."

The doctor smiled down at Uncle Philbert. "How are we feeling today?" he asked.

"I don't know about *you*," said Uncle Philbert, "but

143

I'm feeling kinda spleeny. Had an operation the other day. You mighta heard about it. And my breakfast is being interrupted."

Dr. Haley gave him an irritated look, but then he fished in the pocket of his white lab coat and produced an object that looked like a fat silver dollar with wires protruding from it. He held it out for the less important doctors to view.

"This," he announced, "is an electronic pacemaker. We put one like this in the patient yesterday. It's a surprisingly simple operation—very quick and easy."

Putting down his fork, Uncle Philbert plucked the object out of Dr. Haley's hand and examined it suspiciously.

Dr. Haley gave him a benevolent smile. "From now on," he said to Uncle Philbert, in a voice that a kindergarten teacher might use after she'd finished putting a Band-Aid on a boo-boo, "you'll be right as rain."

"Huh," sniffed Uncle Philbert. "Right as rain. Who says rain is right? It ain't if you got a hay crop to get in."

Dr. Haley ignored him. "Any questions?" he asked. It was clear this was directed at the medical students, but Parker put up his hand.

"How do you adjust its speed—the pacemaker's speed?"

Dr. Haley looked put out for a moment. "We have a sort of remote control device," he said shortly. "Other questions?"

"Awesome," said Parker. He smiled at the thought of Uncle Philbert—Mr. Phooey-to-Technology—being run by a remote control. "Does it have fast-forward? Slow-mo?"

Uncle Philbert raised his hand, waving the pacemaker in the air. "I got a question. How much does one of these little doodads run you?"

"Uh . . . ah," said Dr. Haley. "Well, you'll have to take that up with the billing department. They cost a pretty penny—maybe twenty thousand."

"*Twenty thousand dollars?*" Uncle Philbert whistled. "For this little doohickey? Is that parts and labor? Or just parts?"

"No, no. My fee is not included in that. But I think—"

Uncle Philbert interrupted again. "Does that include batteries? For that amount o' money, they sure better toss in a couple o' double A's at least."

"It does come with a battery that—"

"Good," said Uncle Philbert. "Because I was gonna say, plugging me into an extension cord, that would be a tad awkward. Now then, what's the warranty on this little item? Five years or fifty thousand miles—whichever comes first? Or is it a lifetime guarantee? A lifetime *money-back* guarantee? And if so, is that *my* lifetime? Would that mean that if I croak, I get all my money back? Or—"

Parker stuck his hand up again. Without waiting to be called on, he said, "Dr. Haley? That remote control thingy? Does it by any chance come with a shut-up button?"

"Shut up, *please*," came a familiar scratchy voice from Uncle Philbert's bedside.

Dr. Haley—and the whole flock of junior doctors—looked from Uncle Philbert to Parker to the bedside table that had apparently just spoken. But before they could react, Dr. Haley's pager went off. He pulled it out, frowned at it, tried to silence it, shook it, and said, "That's odd," as it continued to shriek.

"Runcible," hissed Aunt Mattie under her breath, addressing the bedside table, "you stop that!"

Uncle Philbert carried on as if there had been no interruption. "I sure hope it's a lifetime guarantee because this one"—he held up the demo model Haley had given him—"this one don't seem to be workin' so good anymore."

With some annoyance Dr. Haley put his pager away and snatched the pacemaker back from Uncle Philbert, who had been holding it up to his ear and shaking it. The doctor frowned and peered at it.

"Funny," he said, tapping it a few times. "It was working a moment ago. What did you do to it?" He glared at Uncle Philbert, who exchanged a knowing glance with Aunt Mattie. "This thing's worth a small fortune and—" Dr. Haley held the pacemaker up to his own ear, but just then the pacemaker—or something—made a series of wild popping sounds. Just like kernels of popcorn exploding.

Dr. Haley jumped and hastily placed the pacemaker in his pocket. Then he cleared his throat and tried to resume his air of dispensing important information. He turned to Aunt Mattie. "Now then, Mrs. uh—"

"Maxwell."

"Mrs. Maxwell, you may have heard that you are not

146

supposed to use microwave ovens and many electronic appliances around a pacemaker. You must have been worrying about this."

Aunt Mattie, who had removed some wool and needles from her purse at the start of this conversation, glanced up from her knitting. "Oh, I suppose I must," she said solemnly.

"Well, you will be glad to know that, these days, it is perfectly safe to use your microwave around a pacemaker. And your cell phone. Your PDA. Your wireless Internet. In fact, your whole telecommunications system." He beamed. "All are safe to use."

"Well *thank goodness* for that!" said Uncle Philbert, giving Aunt Mattie a secret wink. "Because I was about to say: No cell phone, no pacemaker. It's a whatsit, a—"

"A deal breaker?" supplied Parker, who'd heard his father use the term often.

Uncle Philbert nodded. "A deal breaker. And, listen, what about my lawn mower *system*? Is that safe? Because it would be nice to have a doctor's note saying I wasn't allowed to mow the—"

But Dr. Haley had had enough. "Now if you don't mind," he said, pulling out a stethoscope, "I'd like to demonstrate—"

"But I do mind," said Uncle Philbert, looking longingly at his cake. "I'm feeling a bit . . . What's a word that describes how you feel when you've just been told you're gonna be right as rain but poor as a pauper?"

"Scumbly?" suggested Parker, with a small smile.

"Yes, scumbly," said his great-uncle. "The very word.

I am feeling a tad *scumbly* just now. And hungry. So if *you* don't mind—"

"Scumbly?" repeated Dr. Haley. He took a closer look at Uncle Philbert. Parker noticed for the first time that his great-uncle had turned bright red and was starting to perspire. Dr. Haley pressed the call button for the nurse, and moments later Mrs. Bellwether showed up at a run.

"Why didn't you tell me that the patient is *spiking a fever*?" snapped Dr. Haley.

Mrs. Bellwether placed a hand on Uncle Philbert's forehead.

"D*o*bon't w*o*borro*b*y. It's just the ch*o*bilo*b*i," explained Uncle Philbert.

"*And* he's babbling and hallucinating!" added Dr. Haley. He pulled out a penlight and shone it into Uncle Philbert's eyes. "Get him down to Intensive Care!"

Mrs. Bellwether took a certain pleasure in patting Dr. Haley on the wrist and telling him not to panic, the patient was perfectly "f*o*bine." Which, of course, he was.

"Chili always makes me sweat," Uncle Philbert told the great man. "Beans, on the other hand, always make—"

But, sadly for Dr. Haley, before he could discover the effect of beans on Uncle Philbert, the doctor's pager appeared to go off again. He pulled the gizmo off his belt and squinted at it in confusion. Finally he grunted and put his stethoscope away. "Gotta run. I'm afraid I'm a very busy man." He herded his small flock out the door, muttering as he left, "I really must get that pager looked at."

"I was afraid he'd never leave," said Uncle Philbert. "I used to think *I* was rude, but that guy can run circles around me." Just then the bag beside the bed spoke again.

"Say *thank you*," it squawked.

"Thank you, Runcible," Uncle Philbert said.

...Rudest!

Once they were alone, Uncle Philbert lay back in bed with a happy sigh. "You know, it's real nice, this hospital," he said to Parker, who was busy investigating all the tubes and wires running into and out of his great-uncle. "They set you up with everything you need. I don't have to lift a finger. Look here." He raised his right hand, which had a tube in it that ran up a pole to a plastic bag full of what looked like water. "This here is my very own *personal hydration system*. Even better than Mr. Numitz's. I can drink without having to open my mouth. And this"—he tapped the narrow plastic tubes that ran from his nostrils to a machine next to the bed—"is my *personal oxygenation system*. Can breathe air without having to actually suck in and out." Then he gestured toward yet another tube carrying a pale yellow liquid to a plastic bag at the foot of the bed. "As for this, it's my own *personal drainage system*. I don't even have to get out of bed to take a—"

"Philbert," said Aunt Mattie. "That's enough of that. Otherwise we'll get your remote control and press the ... What did you call it, dear?" she asked Parker.

"The mute button," said Parker. But he grinned at his great-uncle. "Gotta keep it PG-13, Uncle Philbert."

"Right, boss," said Uncle Philbert with a wink. "Whatever that means. Now, Mattie, let's see what else you've got in that suitcase you call a purse."

So they unpacked the Scrabble set and let Runcible out of her little traveling cage. She climbed onto Philbert's tray table and began sampling the crackers that came with the chili.

A few moments later there was a cheery, rapid knock on the door and then, without waiting for a response, Mr. Numitz entered the room with a sunny smile and a showy bouquet of flowers.

"Mr. Maxwell," he said. "Glad to hear you're doing well." Aunt Mattie and Uncle Philbert stared at him in astonishment.

"How on earth did you know we—" began Aunt Mattie, but Uncle Philbert interrupted her.

"I heard tell of lawyers that was ambulance chasers," he snorted, "but helicopter chasers? What did you do, sprout wings?"

"There was a little write-up in the local paper," Mr. Numitz explained with a jovial smile. "I thought I'd stop in and see how you were doing. I ran into Dr. Haley just now, and he says you're going to be fine."

"I'm curious: what part of the No Visitors sign don't you understand? Is it the *No* or the *Visitors*?"

"Oh, hey," Mr. Numitz said, chuckling, "I'm practically family. I'm looking out for your best interests here." He took a moment to arrange the flower vase on the windowsill and then turned to address the Maxwells. "This is perhaps an awkward subject to raise at this moment, but I wanted to ask you: Have you given any thought to how you're going to pay your medical bills? Cardiac surgeons like Dr. Haley don't come cheap."

"If only I could buy Dr. Haley for what he's worth," muttered Uncle Philbert, "and then sell him for what he *thinks* he's worth. I'd make a killing."

Mr. Numitz gave a stiff little laugh while fishing around in his briefcase. "Ha ha." It was like listening to a laugh track. Runcible clearly appreciated the sound, too.

"Ha ha," she muttered experimentally. "Ha ha! Pop! Pop!"

Mr. Numitz ignored her. "Two things I want to leave you with," he said. He handed Uncle Philbert some papers. "First, I thought you might want another copy of the Purchase and Sale agreement, in case you'd like to reconsider signing it. And second, I'm charged with delivering this letter from my client. It explains that if you refuse to sell your farm, the state will take your land from you by eminent domain."

Uncle Philbert gave him a Look. It was a Look that, had Mr. Numitz been an egg, would have cooked him from the inside out. If looks could microwave, it would have microwaved him in a matter of seconds—pacemaker or no pacemaker.

For once Mr. Numitz seemed to get the message. Perhaps he felt his innards starting to simmer. At any rate, he placed the papers on Uncle Philbert's bed and backed slowly to the door, his smile carefully in place.

152

"I'll just leave you to mull this over, shall I?" And then
he was gone.

A silence descended on the room, broken only by the
clicking of Aunt Mattie's knitting needles.

"Maybe you could sell off a *piece* of the farm, Uncle
Philbert—just a little piece," suggested Parker.

"And maybe I could sell one of my kidneys, too,"
snapped Uncle Philbert. "But I ain't going to. I druther
give the farm away than break it up into little pieces
and sell it off bit by bit."

"There must be something else you could sell," said
Parker, "to raise some money."

"I misdoubt it," said Philbert. "I seriously misdoubt
it."

Parker looked from Aunt Mattie to Uncle Philbert.

153

"I don't know if this will help," he blurted out, reaching into his pocket. He pulled out a wad of bills and set them down on the tray in front of Uncle Philbert. Then he dug around in the other pocket and added some coins. His great-aunt and great-uncle looked from the pile of money to Parker and back again. "It's only $482.36," said Parker, feeling self-conscious. "I mean, it would have been more, but I . . . I had to buy something on the way here."

"Where'd you get *that*?" asked Uncle Philbert after a stunned silence.

"It's my, my . . ." Suddenly the idea of getting a five-hundred-dollar allowance seemed so ridiculous that Parker couldn't bring himself to say it aloud. "My dad gave it to me. For emergencies."

"Well, that's terribly kind of you, dear," said Aunt Mattie, sweeping up the money and handing it back to him. "But you keep it for a real emergency."

What realer emergency was there than this? Parker wondered. You get a heart attack and you have to sell your farm to pay your bills.

"Even if I could raise some money," said Uncle Philbert, scanning the letter Mr. Numitz had left behind, "they've got us with this eminent domain thing."

"What's 'eminent domain'?" It was a term Parker had heard his father use, and he knew it was something nasty.

Uncle Philbert glanced down at the letter. "It appears to mean that the state can force you to sell them your land, willy-nilly. I think they've got us by the short hairs." He tossed the letter and stared at the food on his table. At last he looked over at Aunt Mattie and cleared his throat.

"I hear tell that Florida is nice in the winters, Matilda. Sunny and—"

"That is utter and complete claptrap. I'm surprised at you, Philbert Maxwell," snapped Aunt Mattie. "Sunny, my left foot."

Parker had never heard her sound so fierce. He turned to his great-uncle. "Yeah," he said. "What a crate of flapdoodle." He bent over and took the last item out of Aunt Mattie's purse. *"Illegitimi non carborundum,"* he said, offering the baseball cap to his great-uncle. "Right, Uncle Philbert?"

Uncle Philbert turned the cap over in his hand several times. At last he nodded, and settled the cap on his head, pulling the brim down hard.

"Darn straight," he said to Parker. "Now where's that Right-Side-Up Cake? I could eat a horse, right side up, upside down, or inside out."

Caped Crusader to the Rescue

That night Parker went owling around once again. He opened closets and cupboards. He poked around the kitchen and the living room. He checked under sofa cushions. This time he wasn't looking for hidden television sets or something to eat. He wasn't exactly sure what he was looking for. He only knew he didn't find it.

Back in his room, he lay in bed, unable to sleep and trying to think.

So much old junk. He just *knew* that some of it had to be worth something. He hadn't spent hundreds of hours surfing the Internet and cruising eBay not to know the fortunes people would happily pay for old stuff. There had to be something of value here that they could sell. Something as valuable as a kidney, or a piece of the land, but that wouldn't hurt so much to part with. What, though? As far as he could tell, most of the furniture really *was* junk, and anything that might truly be an antique had long since been destroyed by cats using it as a scratching post. As for the rest of the stuff the place was bursting with, he doubted even the most avid collector would be interested in wooden tennis rackets without strings, or the 1958 phone book for Schenectady, New York.

At last, he pulled *Batman and Robin* off the bedside table and read until he fell asleep, the comic book resting gently on his chin, the bedside light still on.

In his dream, the Batmobile is a familiar black New York taxicab with bat wings instead of doors. He is dressed as Robin, and Batman looks suspiciously like Uncle Philbert, except that, instead of a silver mustache, he has silver oxygen tubes coming out of his nose.

"Where's my dang-blasted mustache gone?" he asks Parker. "It's extremely valuable."

"Holy facial hair, Batman!" says Parker. "It's right under your nose." He reaches over to show him.

The movement jerked him awake and he lay there for a moment, blinking in the light of the bedside lamp and watching the goldfish. Then he started to laugh. Because he just realized that the answer *was* right under his nose—literally. He'd just been too stupid to see it.

What Century Is This, Again?

The day they picked up Uncle Philbert was a cool, end-of-summer day, the sky crisp and blue. It was the kind of day Parker used to hate because it was full of reminders that school was right around the corner. Today, however, he was concentrating on getting the chores done so that when Uncle Philbert came back he would notice that the wood box was full, the animals fed, the "lawn" perfectly "mowed."

He did the chores with a heavy heart, however. The pleasure he'd felt at solving Aunt Mattie and Uncle Philbert's money problems last night had evaporated by the time the sun rose. Parker had noticed before that brilliant ideas he had in the middle of the night often seemed ridiculous in the harsh light of day. His brainstorm of last night might just be a pipe dream. He needed a way to check it out. What was worse, though, was the realization that even if he solved the money problem, he had no idea what to do about the other problem facing his great-aunt and great-uncle: the land and the eminent domain thing. Still, it was progress, he told himself as he filled the wood box. He was halfway there—he hoped.

When he was finished, he told Aunt Mattie that he had to stop at the mall on the way to the hospital—to pick up that thing he'd ordered the other day.

"It'll be ready by now," he said by way of explanation. Which was partially true.

One of the things he liked best about Aunt Mattie was that she didn't ask him any questions, so he didn't have to lie to her. Now she just nodded and said she had some errands to run, too.

Once she deposited him at the mall, he picked up the hat he'd ordered two days ago, checked out the slogan embroidered on the top, and had to admit it looked great. Then he set off on his real quest.

Somewhere, somewhere, there had to be a computer he could use. He tried the arcade. Nothing. Just stupid games. Next, the video game store. Lots of computers set up, but all playing dumb games. No Internet connection anywhere. He stormed out, without even stopping to try the newest Xbox game. Next stop, the vast office supply store. Dozens of computers, including a few hooked up to the Internet. But when he asked the salesman if he could use one, all he got was a dirty look.

Strike three. He was out of ideas. And thoroughly disgusted.

Was it so much to ask—twenty minutes of Internet access? He could understand his great-aunt and great-uncle not having a computer. After all, they were practically born in the nineteenth century. But how was it possible that in this entire twenty-first-century mall, there was not a single computer connected to the Internet?

He slumped into the front seat of the car. Aunt Mattie gave him a kindly look but refrained from asking questions, for which he was, once again, grateful. He tried not to sulk on the way to the hospital, tried not to mind when Aunt Mattie detoured to stop at the local library to return some books. Tried not to grunt when she asked if he'd like to come in, too. Resisted reminding her that the only thing he read was comics and the last time he checked, libraries didn't carry comics. Refrained from telling her that libraries were *so* last century. Until he remembered.

Libraries have computers. Computers hooked up to the Internet. For anyone to use. He was out the door in a flash.

Different

In the happiness of seeing Uncle Philbert installed at the kitchen table—a bit paler, perhaps, but full of vinegar—with Fraidy Cat on his lap as if he had never left, neither Parker nor anyone else heard the car pull up outside the front door.

His great-aunt and great-uncle were playing Scrabble, and Parker was trying to work out how to say "How does your corporosity seem to gashiate?" in Ob. Even harder, he was trying to figure out how to answer it correctly ("Very discombobulate, great congruity, dissimilarity"). He'd gotten halfway through *discombobulate* (do*b*isco*b*omb*ob*ob—) when he heard the sound of voices on the front veranda.

The door opened, and there was a moment of shocked silence all around.

"Mom," said Parker, rising to his feet. "Dad. What are you doing here?" They stared at each other for a second, then Parker's mother gave a laugh and rushed over to hug him.

"Parker, darling, did you forget we were coming today? We called and called, but no one ever answered the phone. Or your cell." She pushed Parker away, still holding on to his shoulders, and looking at him as if she'd never seen him before. "You look so . . . different."

No, thought Parker, *you* do. His parents seemed somehow . . . smaller. With a slight shock, he realized he was taller than his mother, that he needed to look down a bit to meet her eyes. And his father, well, he just didn't quite *loom* in the way he used to. More amazing, he looked different. Tanned. Relaxed. The business suit was gone. He was wearing some really dorktastic plaid shorts and a T-shirt that said "Kiss Me, I'm Irish." He stood there, with an arm around Parker's mother's waist, and stuck out a hand for Parker to shake. Parker looked at it and went to high-five his father. His father, without missing a beat, went to high-five him, and Parker stuck out his hand to shake. They did this three times in a row. His father smiled—a smile that went from his mouth to his eyes and back—then threw both hands up in the air and gave Parker a quick hug instead.

"How was your trip?" asked Aunt Mattie. "How was Alaska?"

"Alaska?" repeated Dad. "Very white, Alaska."

"And Greenland?"

His parents exchanged a smile, as if at a private joke. "Greenland?" said Mom. "Very green."

Uncle Philbert nodded approvingly. "Your corporosity seems to be gashiating very discombobulately," he pronounced.

This was followed by a flurry of apologies over having forgotten that Parker's parents were coming, explanations of Uncle Philbert's hospitalization, expressions of dismay, reassurances, and on and on. Watching them all, Parker backed silently out of the kitchen.

"I'll just go get packed," he said at last, but no one seemed to notice, so he ran up the stairs to his room. Once there, he threw his suitcase on the bed and tossed his clothes in. It took only a few moments to pack—he'd brought hardly any clothes. Most of the suitcase had been filled with junk food and video games. When he was packed, he decided, for some reason, to change into the clothes he had come in. He dug out the jeans he hadn't worn since that first day. It was strange to see that the cuffs no longer dragged on the ground. Nor did the waist pinch. In fact, he had to hunt around for a belt to keep the jeans from sliding off him.

Plopping his suitcase next to the stairs, he paused to get his jacket from a hall closet. On the back of the door was a full-length mirror. There were no real mirrors in the rest of the farmhouse. Now, looking at himself for the first time all summer, he saw why it was that his parents had hardly recognized him. For a brief instant he wasn't sure he recognized himself—and if there's any odder sensation than not recognizing your own reflection, Parker didn't want to know it. Gone was the pasty, pudgy kid who had last looked back at him from a mirror. All the freckles on his arms and face had run together in a farmer's tan—a tan that stopped abruptly at his T-shirt. His red hair had grown out from the buzz cut, and the top layer had turned to gold where the sun had bleached it. Even the face looking back at him was different in some way he couldn't put his finger on: longer maybe, thinner certainly. But it wasn't just the tan, the absence of baby fat. It was . . .

He blinked and the sensation of strangeness vanished. The face in the mirror once again seemed utterly familiar. But just as he turned away he noticed something both odd and familiar at the same time. At the corners of his eyes were faint crow's-feet—not wrinkles, like old people had, but pale lines where the tan hadn't reached. His father's eyes now had the same pale crow's-feet around them. They must come from squinting in the sun. Or maybe even, he thought, from smiling.

A Crate of Lies

When he returned to the kitchen, his mother and Aunt Mattie were having an animated conversation about knitting patterns. Uncle Philbert and his father were deep in discussion as well.

"How does that go again?" Dad was asking. "Very discom—"

"—bobulate," said Uncle Philbert. "Great congruity. Dissimilarity."

"Or, in Ob," said Parker, "do*bis*co*bomb*o*bob*ulo*b*ate, gro*b*eat—"

"Don't confuse the man," said Uncle Philbert.

"One thing at a time," said Dad with a smile, rising from the kitchen table. "Okay. Ready to go, buddy?"

"Sure."

As his father stood up, his eye fell on the stack of legal letters that had accumulated in Uncle Philbert's absence. "Franklin Numitz?" he said, looking at one.

"Numbnuts," clarified Runcible.

"The man's a snake. Why are Numitz Bilkum & Smattering writing to you?"

Parker sighed. He had hoped to leave without raising the sad subject of what would become of the farm. No one had mentioned it since that day in the hospital, and Parker had come to understand that it was helpful sometimes to pretend certain stuff didn't exist. Bad stuff you couldn't change. No point in talking about it if you couldn't change it.

Uncle Philbert didn't seem to want to talk about it, either, but he shoved the letters toward Parker's father and said, "You can read 'em for yourself." Parker's father arranged the papers in a neat stack and put on his reading glasses.

"So where do they want to put this turnpike ramp?" he asked, once he'd finished the letters. Uncle Philbert pulled a map from a drawer and pointed out their location.

"There's a good view of it from that hill," said Parker. "If you're interested."

"Yes. I'm very interested. Can we have a look?"

Uncle Philbert nodded. "I'd love to go, but I've got this cat on my lap." Since Uncle Philbert's return, Fraidy Cat had not budged from his lap and certainly looked as if he had no intention of letting Uncle Philbert out of his sight ever again. "Parker can show you the way."

"All right. Let's go, buddy," said his father. Parker grabbed a few things from the defective-sports-equipment closet. His father scooped his car keys off the kitchen table, but Parker stopped him.

"We have to walk there," he explained. "It's not that far." Dad looked at the distant ridge, and back at Parker. He couldn't hide the surprise in his eyes.

"You want to *walk* there?" he asked. Parker nodded. Dad looked uncertainly at Mom and Aunt Mattie. Their conversation had shifted from mittens to motorcycles, and he heard Mom saying, in her most sincere voice, that she would love to have a look at the motorcycle that Aunt Mattie had just finished rebuilding. "Okay, then," he said to Parker. "Lead on."

At the base of the water tower, Parker saw something glinting on the ground and bent to pick it up. It was a fragment of his cell phone.

"That would explain why you weren't answering your phone," Dad said with a wry look.

"Yeah," said Parker. "The Game Boy had a . . . similar accident."

"What happened to it? Somebody throw it out the car window?"

Parker laughed and then told him the whole story of Uncle Philbert's heart attack. His father listened silently.

"Let me get this straight. You *ran* up this hill—without your inhaler," he repeated, shaking his head slightly. "Please don't tell your mother. On second thought, maybe you *should* tell your mother. And then you climbed up *there*?" He craned his neck to look up at the tower looming above them.

"Sure," said Parker. "We have to climb it now, to get a view over the trees. If you want. If you have the time," he added. Stupid question. Dad was almost always in a hurry.

"Sure," Dad said, swallowing hard. "Yes. Why not?

Sure. I've got plenty of time. Time is what I have plenty of."

Parker went first up the ladder. He climbed swiftly up to the halfway platform. Looking down, he saw his father moving one rung at a time: Up, stop. Up, stop. His father saw him looking and gave him a quick wave, before grabbing the ladder again. It was something of a shock for Parker to realize that his father was frightened—actually afraid—of climbing the water tower. How could this be? he wondered. And what had happened to his own fear of heights? He looked down and noticed that his knees were shaking—shaking pretty hard, in fact, though not as hard as last time. His heart, too, was beating fast. So he was still scared of heights—who wasn't, really?—but not *frightened* by them. And there was a world of difference between those two things.

Dad made it up to the halfway platform and stood there, his back pressed against the side of the tower, his hand gripping the low railing that was supposed to keep you from falling off. He was breathing hard.

"We don't have to go any higher," said Parker. "There's a great view from right here."

Dad looked up to the top of the tower, nodded, and checked his watch. "Sure," he said. "If that's what you want. And it *is* getting kind of late."

Parker led him around to the side of the tower where you could see the farm, the mall, and the turn-pike all laid out below them. He pointed out where the neighbors lived, where the ramp was supposed to go—right through the trout pool—how the farm would be sliced up, paved over, ruined. His father relaxed his grip on the railing, and frowned. He made Parker repeat to him where exactly the ramp was to go. Then he began to chuckle.

"Those sly dogs," he said. "It was worth a try, but it will never fly."

"What?" said Parker. "What do you mean?"

"That eminent domain thing was just a bluff. They were trying to take advantage of an old man—betting that he was not the kind of person to lawyer up. Because any lawyer could have told you that."

"Can you talk English, please?"

"Well, look here," he said, putting one hand on Parker's shoulder and using the other to point out what he meant. "The law says you can't take a piece of land by eminent domain—you can't *force* someone to sell their land against their will—unless you don't have any other place you can put your road. Clearly, the shortest and easiest place to put the ramp is straight through the middle of the farm and the neighbor's land. But they could also loop the ramp around the edge of the farm. That ramp would have to be longer, so it'll cost a lot more. That's why the state didn't want to put it there. But it would spare the farm for sure. And the neighbor's land, too."

"But the neighbors *wanted* to sell out. They were going to make a pile of money."

His father gave him a wicked look. "I'm afraid that this way, the ramp won't need to go through their land. It will just go right by their front door—sadly for them." When he saw Parker's puzzled look, he explained a bit more. "It will make their land worthless. The state won't *need* to buy it. And since no one wants to live next to a turnpike ramp, no one else will ever want to buy it either."

Parker knew that it was unkind, but he couldn't help smiling.

"That's why everyone was pushing Uncle Philbert so hard to sell," his father continued. "And they were all counting on him not figuring that out."

"So it was just a bluff?" said Parker. "A whopping can of flapdoodle?"

"A whopping can."

"*Yes!*" exclaimed Parker, pounding the side of the water tower with delight and startling his father. He began to laugh. Wait till he told Uncle Philbert. Now both halves of the problem were solved.

On their way back to the farmhouse, though it was growing late and though he was dying to tell Uncle Philbert and Aunt Mattie what his father had said about the turnpike ramp, Parker made a detour to the trout stream.

"I just need to look for something," he explained to his father. Then he took the little fine-meshed net, the one that was used for catching minnows and frogs, and climbed out to the big boulder that had been the Old Baister's favorite spot to laze about. He lay down on his stomach and gazed into the depths of the pool. The water had finally settled back to its clear-as-glass state, and Parker could now see straight to the bottom. A grin spread over his face, and he reached out care-

fully with the net and made a quick pass through the water with it. Lifting the net into the air with a triumphant look, he held it out for his father to see.

Dad frowned, apparently thinking the net was empty. Then he looked more closely. At the bottom of the mesh, three miniature fish—each hardly longer than an inch—flipped about, protesting the sudden change in atmosphere and doing their tiny, fierce level best to get back to the water.

"What are those?" asked Dad. "Baby fish?"

Parker looked closely. Yes, they had the exact right markings, small as they were. "Baby Baisters," corrected Parker. "Tough little just-hatched-out Baisters. By next summer they'll be big enough for me to catch."

His father raised his eyebrows. "Next summer?"

"You bet," said Parker.

Moving Out

"Well, what do you know about *that*?" said Uncle Philbert, putting down the letter he was reading when Parker told him what his father had said about eminent domain. "It was all a complete crate of flapdoodle."

Parker wasn't quite sure what he'd expected Uncle Philbert to do when he heard this news, but he found this response extremely disappointing. Maybe it was too much to expect the old man to punch the air and do a little end-zone victory dance, but still . . . Maybe he hadn't understood.

"Aren't you pleased, Uncle Philbert? Don't you see? This means they can't take your farm away. They can't make you sell it."

"Sure. Pleased as pickles," he said. But he soon went back to frowning at the letter in his hand, and Aunt Mattie chose that moment to make a great deal of noise clearing away dishes. Parker saw that the letter his great-uncle was reading was from the billing department at the hospital. Of course! How could he be so dense?

"You're not still thinking about selling the farm to pay your bills, are you? Because—"

"Parker," interrupted Mom. "It's not polite to discuss—"

"—that would be really, really dumb."

"Parker!" That was Dad getting into the act.

"No, seriously. You don't need to sell the farm to raise money. You're sitting on a gold mine. I—"

The four adults in the room were all staring at him, mouths slightly ajar, as if he'd gone off the deep end.

"I found a way . . ." Parker began, but then figured it would be far easier if he just showed them all what he had found. He bolted from the kitchen and returned in a few minutes with a cardboard box. "There," he said, tossing the box onto the table with a dramatic thud that startled Fraidy Cat so badly he nearly jumped off Uncle Philbert's lap. "There's the solution. Right here under our noses all along."

His father reached into the box. "*Batman and Robin*," he said in a wondering tone. "I used to love those guys." He looked sheepishly at Mom.

"So you found my old comic book collection," said Uncle Philbert with a laugh. "I gave a couple to Simon when he was visiting last spring. You're welcome to them. Aunt Mattie here is always after me to throw them away. You want to take some home with you?"

"No," said Parker, who couldn't help blushing at the memory of how he had "accidentally" destroyed those comics, Simon's comics, the last time he had seen his cousin.

"Please do!" said Mattie. "Bertie's such a dreadful old pack rat. You've no idea how—"

"No!" Parker practically shouted the word. Then he took a moment to pull himself together. Everyone was staring open-mouthed at him once again. "I want you to *sell* them," he continued in a calmer voice. "Then you won't have to sell the farm."

Aunt Mattie and Uncle Philbert chuckled heartily. "I don't think a few comic books are going to pay off my medical bills," said his great-uncle.

But Dad shot Parker a look. "What are you saying, son?"

"I went on the Internet and checked it out. These

175

comics are worth a ton of money—like maybe twenty or thirty thousand dollars. They're all really, really old and really rare. Plus they're in great condition. That one you have is worth almost two thousand dollars."

His father gave a low whistle and looked at the comic he had in his hand. "You're right. Look at this: *Batman No. 1: All Brand New Adventures of the Batman*

and Robin, the Boy Wonder! Spring 1940. It's the very first Batman comic ever written. That's a collector's item if ever I saw one." He picked up a second comic. "*Batman No. 2.* Another beauty. Amazing."

"Well, did you ever!" said Aunt Mattie, looking truly happy.

"What did I tell you, woman?" crowed Uncle Philbert. "I always told her, you never know when some of this junk might come in handy. You think it's enough to pay off Dr. Haley?"

"Sure is," said Parker. "With enough left over for a new tractor, too. And a new—"

"New tractor?" said Aunt Mattie, narrowing her eyes suspiciously. "Bertie, is there something you haven't told me—"

"You found all this on the Interweb?" Uncle Philbert interjected hastily, turning to Parker and trying not to meet Matilda's eye. Parker nodded.

"That's Parker for you," said Good Old Dad proudly. "He's a Boy Wonder on that computer of his."

As they were getting into the car to leave, Uncle Philbert approached Parker's window, clutching Fraidy Cat to his chest, and somehow balancing Runcible on his shoulder. With his free hand he pulled off his *Illegitimi* baseball cap and handed it to Parker.

"I want you to keep this," he said. "Everyone needs a motto."

"Wow," said Parker. "Thanks, Uncle Philbert." On the brim were five of Uncle Philbert's prize trout flies.

"But . . . YOMANC," said Uncle Philbert. Parker gave

him a quizzical look. "Y-O-M-A-N-C," he spelled out. "Means: You Owe Me A New Cap."

Parker laughed out loud and then said, "Wait! I can't believe I almost forgot this." He dug around in his backpack for a second, produced a paper bag, and thrust it out the window.

"Why, what's this?" asked Uncle Philbert, taking the bag.

"Just open it. I . . . It's for you. I had it made."

Uncle Philbert for a change did exactly as he was told. The bag contained a bright orange baseball cap. Embroidered across the front were the words *Semper Ubi Sub Ubi*.

Uncle Philbert squinted a bit, as if trying to remember. "Let's see," he said slowly. "*Semper* is 'always.' *Ubi* is . . . 'where.' *Sub* means 'under.' And—oh, I get it." Uncle Philbert interrupted his translation with a big grin as he figured it out.

"I suck at Latin," said Parker quickly. "I probably got it all wrong. But I thought you needed a new motto. Like the Marines. You know, *Semper Fi*."

"Just exactly like the Marines," said Uncle Philbert. "Only different."

"My mom always says you have to be prepared," said Parker, in a low voice meant only for Uncle Philbert's ears. "In case you end up in the emergency room."

"Which I ain't ever doin' again," said Uncle Philbert, tapping his chest proudly. " 'Cause I got the best little *cardiac control system* that comic books can buy. Lifetime warranty. And anyone who says otherwise can just eat my shorts. Ain't that so, Runcible?"

Runcible fixed him with her beadiest glare. "Do my chores," she corrected, in her new prim and proper voice. "Please."

Everyone laughed, and Parker looked over at his father, who nodded his head a few times, as if trying to recall something. Suddenly he grinned at Parker. "Atomic batteries to power," he said, flicking on the ignition. "Turbines to speed."

"Roger, Batman," said Parker. "Ready to move out."

GLOSSARY

Mattie and Philbert use a lot of words you won't find in most dictionaries. Here are my attempts to provide definitions.

corporosity: "How does your *corporosity* seem to *gashiate*?" is Mattie's way of saying "How are you?" It's an expression that she thinks she made up, using invented words, but what she doesn't know is that my mother used to ask me this same question every morning at breakfast, and *her* mother did the same to her.

The answer to this peculiar question ("Very *discombobulate*. Great *congruity*. *Dissimilarity*") is also nonsense—but at least it uses real words. You'll have to go to the dictionary to find out what *they* mean.

dozey: Rotten. It's only used to refer to wood. Hamlet, for example, would never say, "Something is dozey in the state of Denmark."

druther: Comes from jamming *would rather* together and saying it fast. Your *druthers* are something you *druther* have, if you had a choice—which you usually don't. Because you're just a kid and life isn't fair.

flapdoodle: Nonsense. *Flapdoodle* has a nicer ring to it, though. See also *folderol*.

folderol: See *flapdoodle*.

fub: To mess up, or mess around with something.

fummydiddle: To *fub*. (*Fummydiddle* is for people who prefer to use longer, more impressive-sounding words.)

gashiate: See *corporosity*.

gormy: Dull-witted and clumsy.

hay-burner: A gas-guzzler, only with four legs and a tail.

hole in the snow: Worthless—like a hole in the snow. Kind of a crass expression, if you think about how that hole got in that snow.

hornswoggle: Bamboozle. Hoax.

jeezly: Darned.

jizzicked: Beyond repair. Ruined.

misdoubt: This means to *really* doubt something.

palaver: Pointless, long-winded talk.

scumbly: Feeling good and bad at the same time. Sometimes Parker just makes up words because he likes to cheat at Scrabble. Deal with it.

weewaw: Crooked. Used only to describe things that are *supposed* to be straight or vertical. So, for example, your front steps could be *weewaw*, but you wouldn't say a bolt of lightning was *weewaw*. You might say, "There was a *weewaw* man / and he walked a *weewaw* mile," but people would look at you funny.

whiffet: A small, young, or unimportant person. Or so claims Uncle Philbert (see *No More Nasty*).

HCOLX +
MACDO

MACDONALD, AMY
    TOO MUCH FLAPDOODLE!

COLLIER
05/09